# Just Another Morning

By LINDA ASHMAN
Illustrated by CLAUDIO MUÑOZ

HarperCollins Publishers

Just Another Morning

Manufactured in China by South China Printing Company Ltd.
 www.harperchildrens.com

---

Library of Congress Cataloging-in-Publication Data
Ashman, Linda.
Just another morning / by Linda Ashman ; illustrated by Claudio Muñoz.— 1st ed.
p. cm.
Summary: A little boy imagines that the everyday objects around him are fantastic creatures as he goes about his day.
ISBN 0-06-029053-6 — ISBN 0-06-029054-4 (lib. bdg.)
[1. Day—Fiction. 2. Stories in rhyme.] I. Muñoz, Claudio, ill. II. Title.
PZ8.3.A775Ju 2004 2003006320
[E]—dc21

---

Typography by Elynn Cohen 1 2 3 4 5 6 7 8 9 10
❖ First Edition

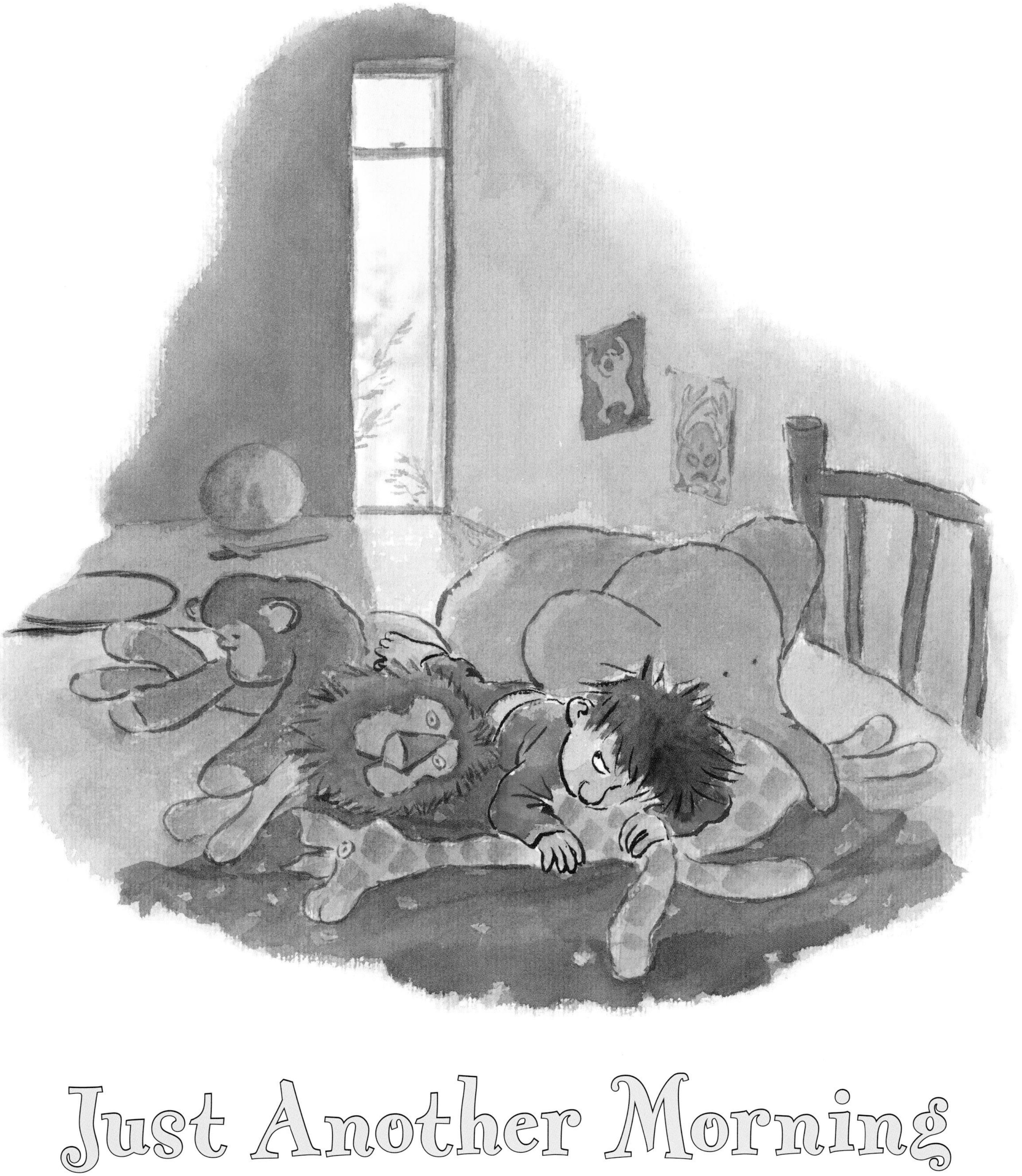

# Just Another Morning

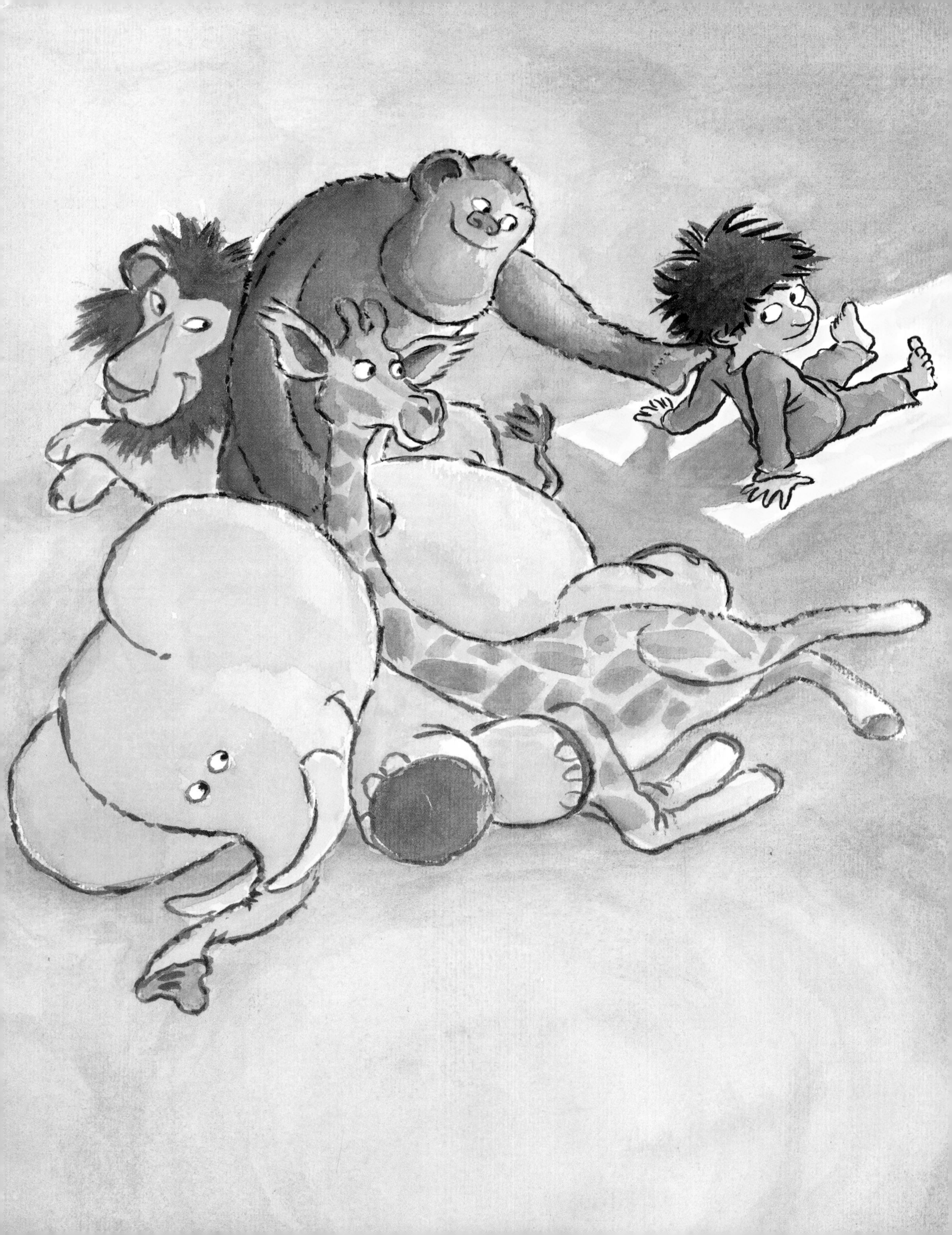

The day begins as many do:
I find myself inside a zoo.

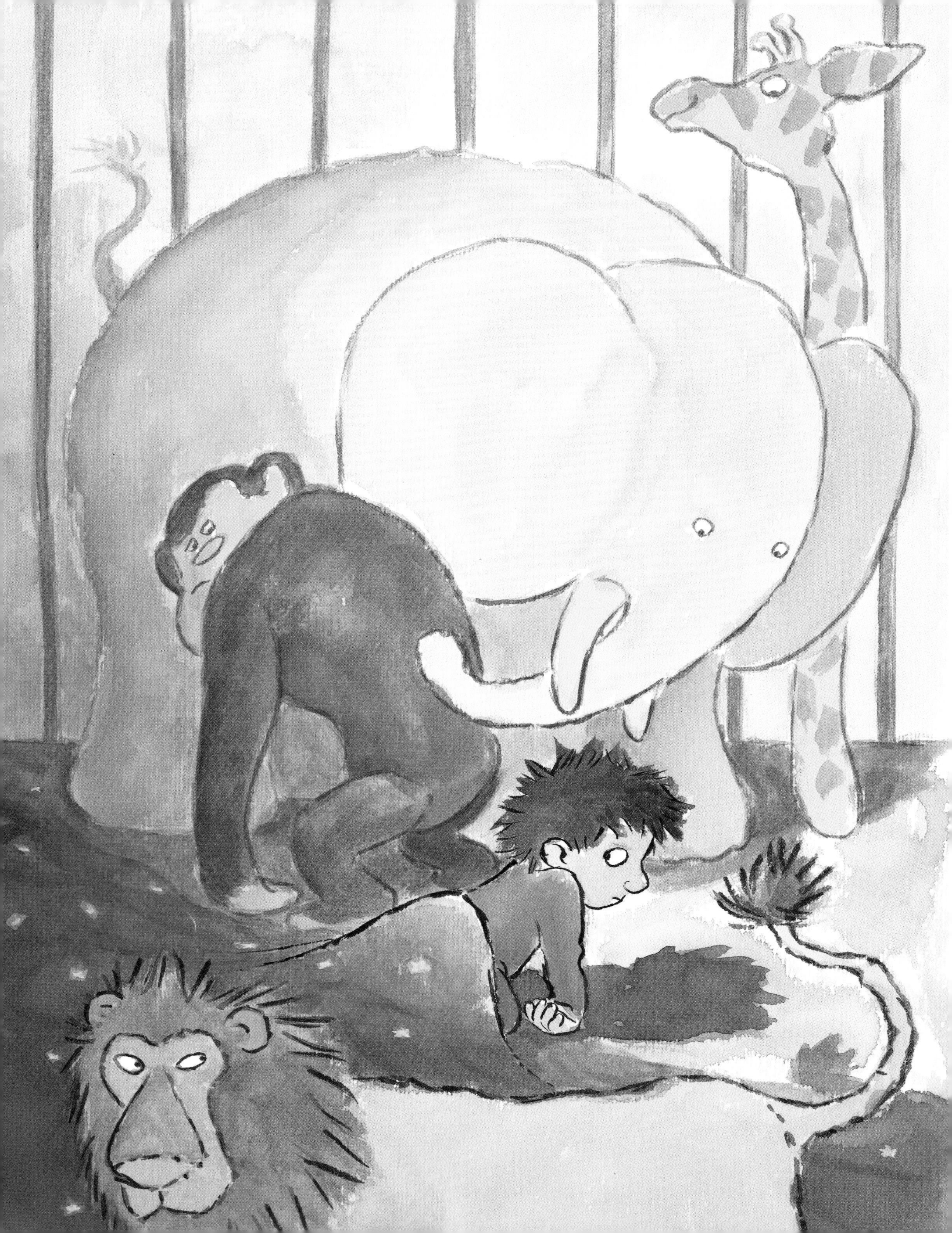

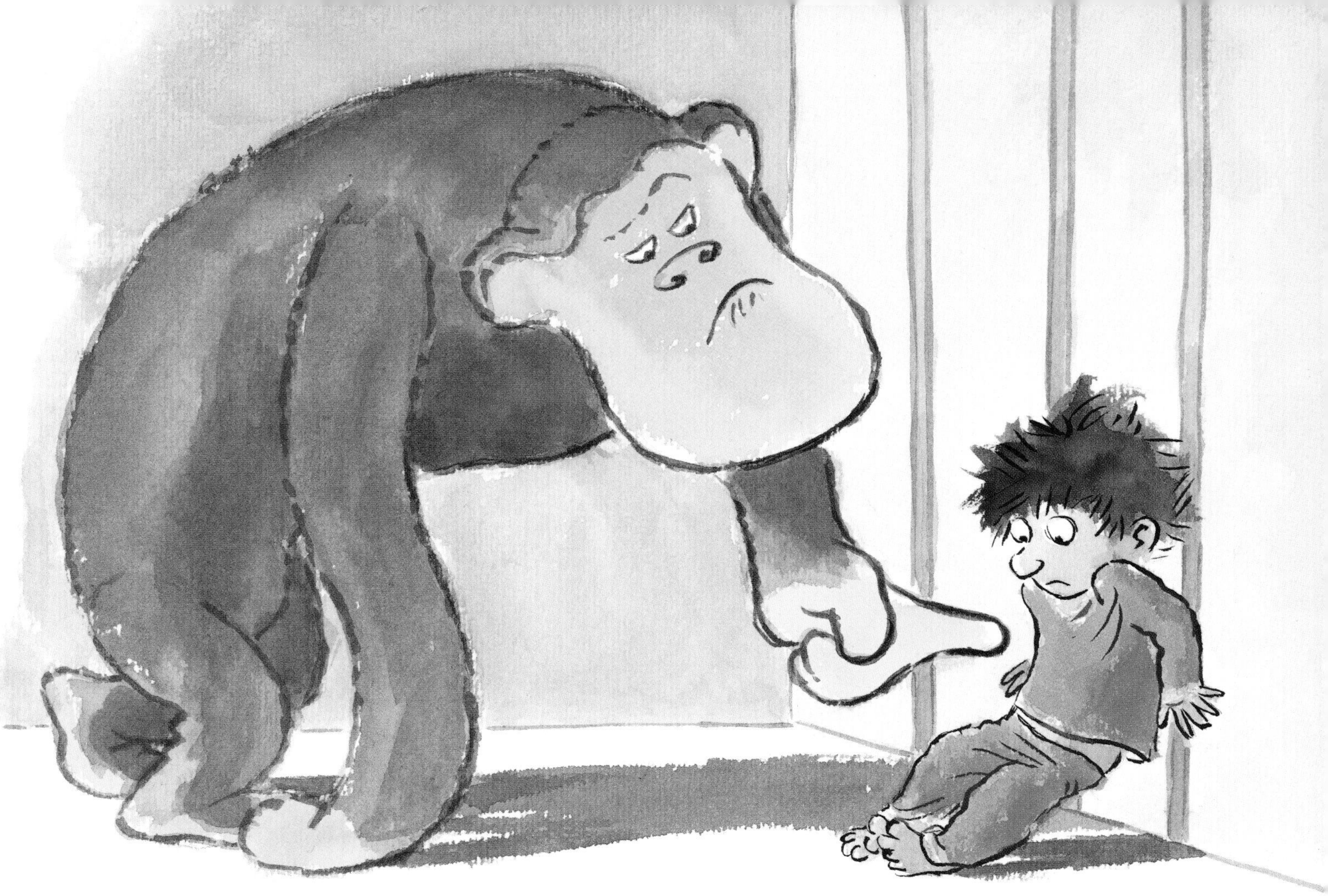

I'm cornered by a savage ape—
I growl and make a quick escape.

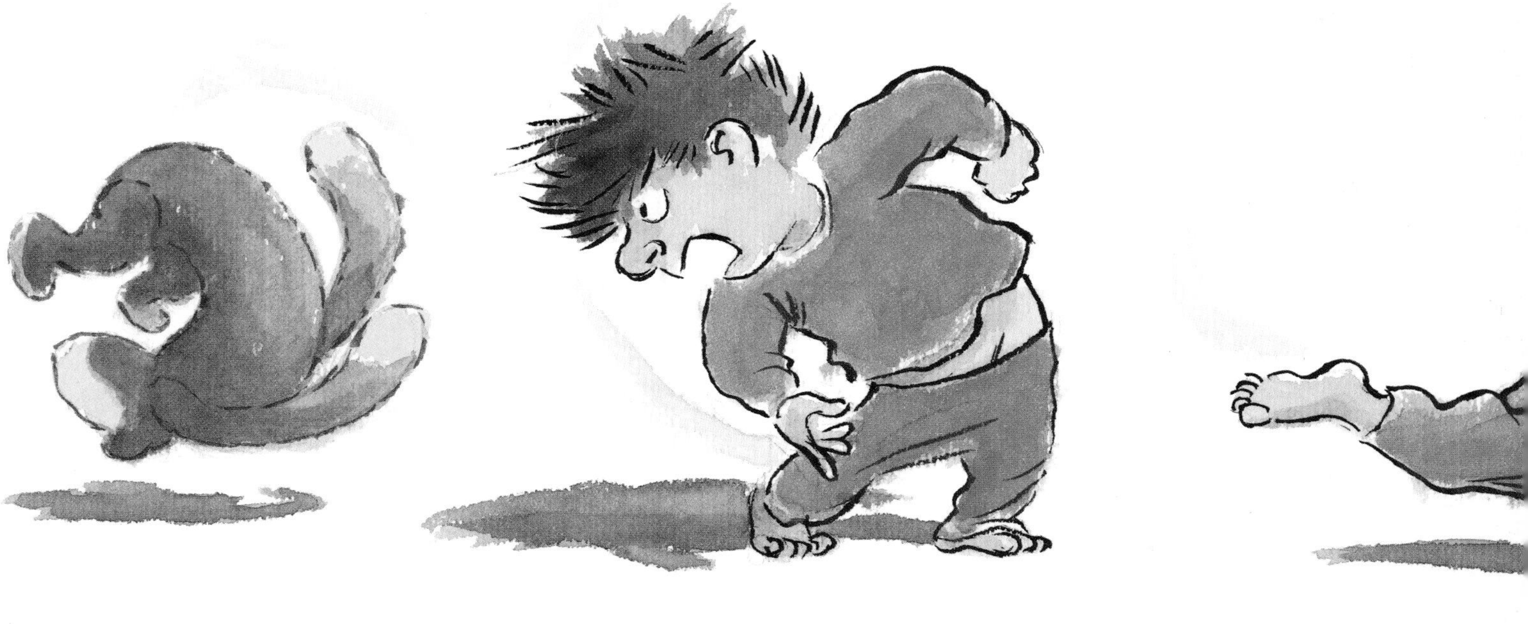

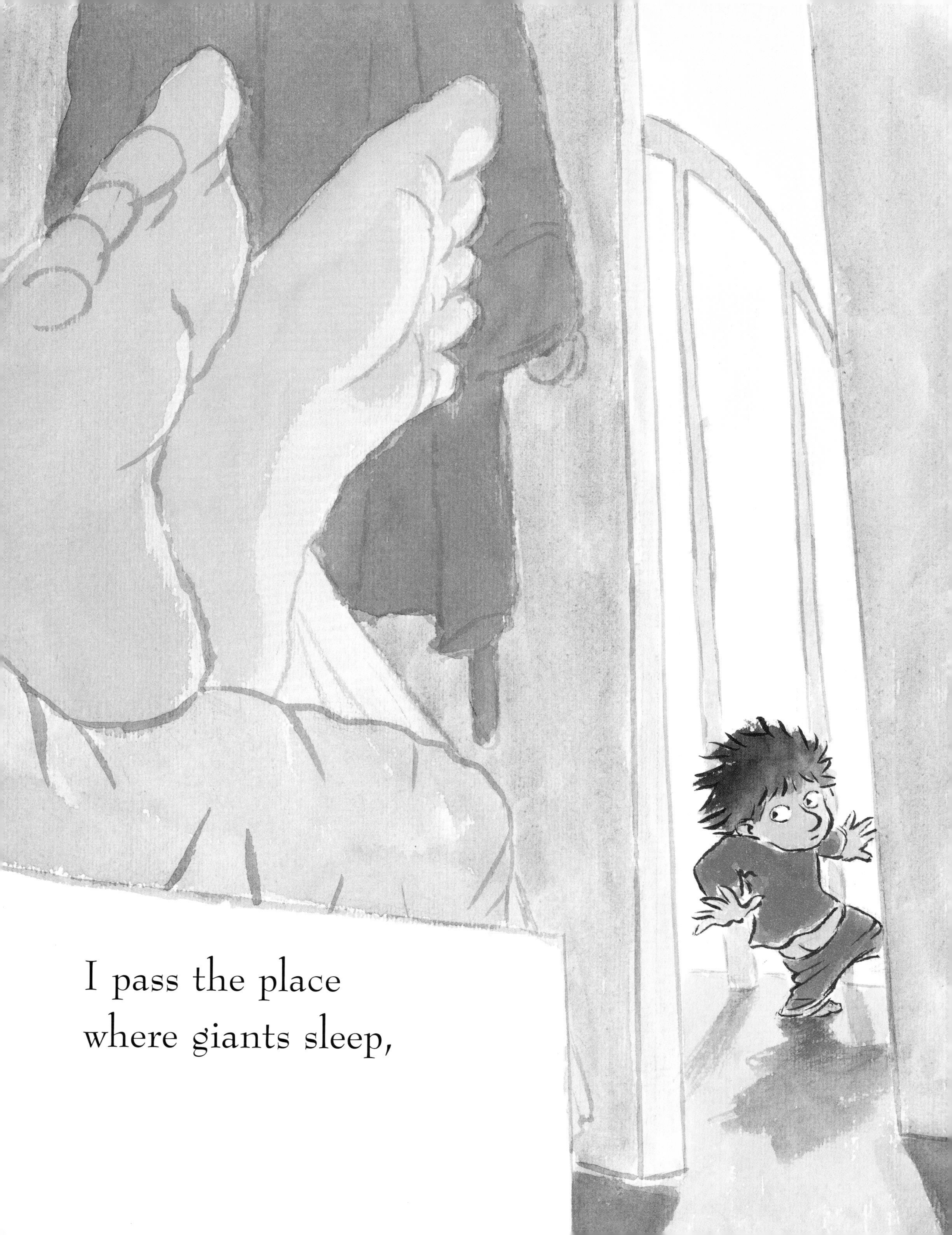

I pass the place
where giants sleep,

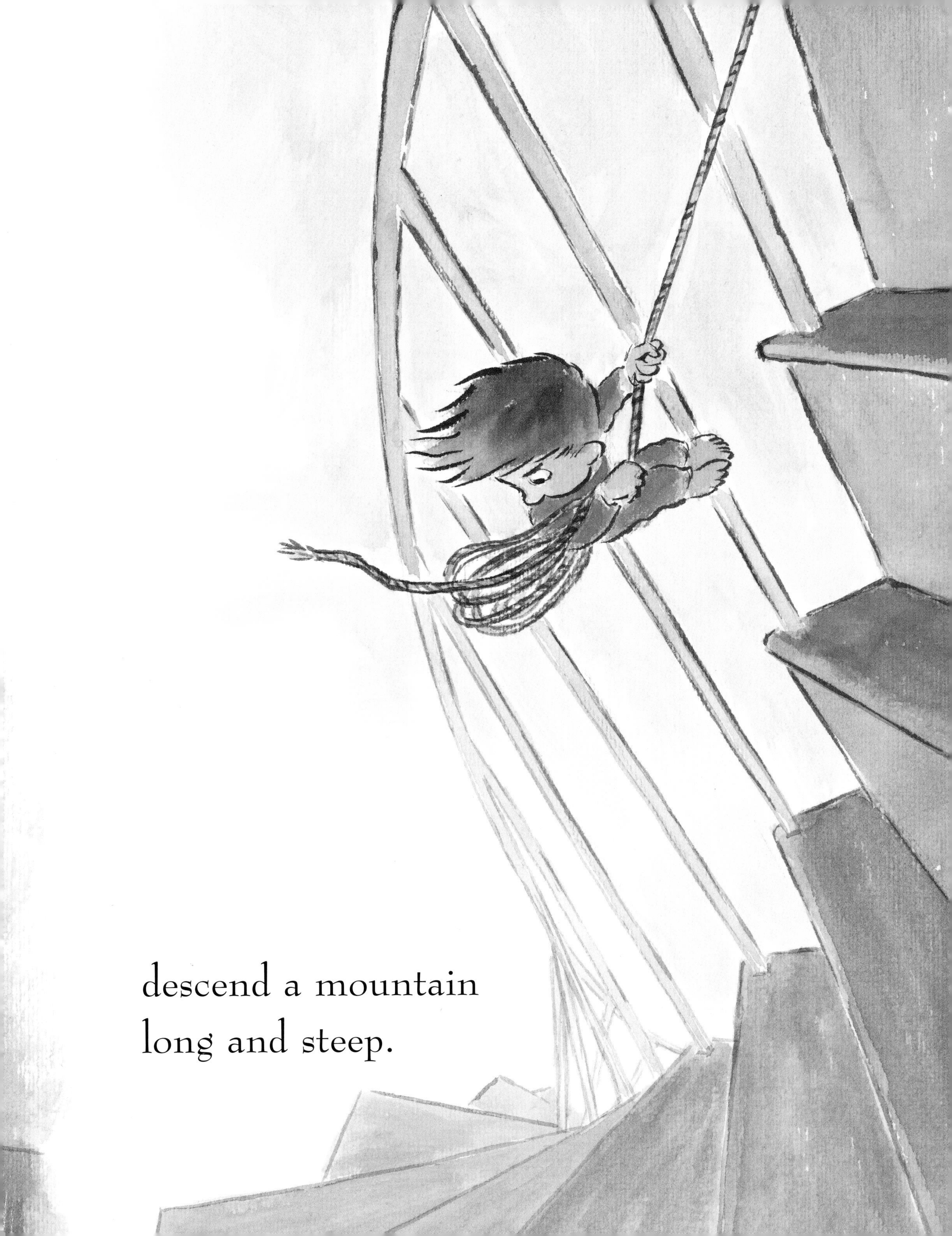

descend a mountain
long and steep.

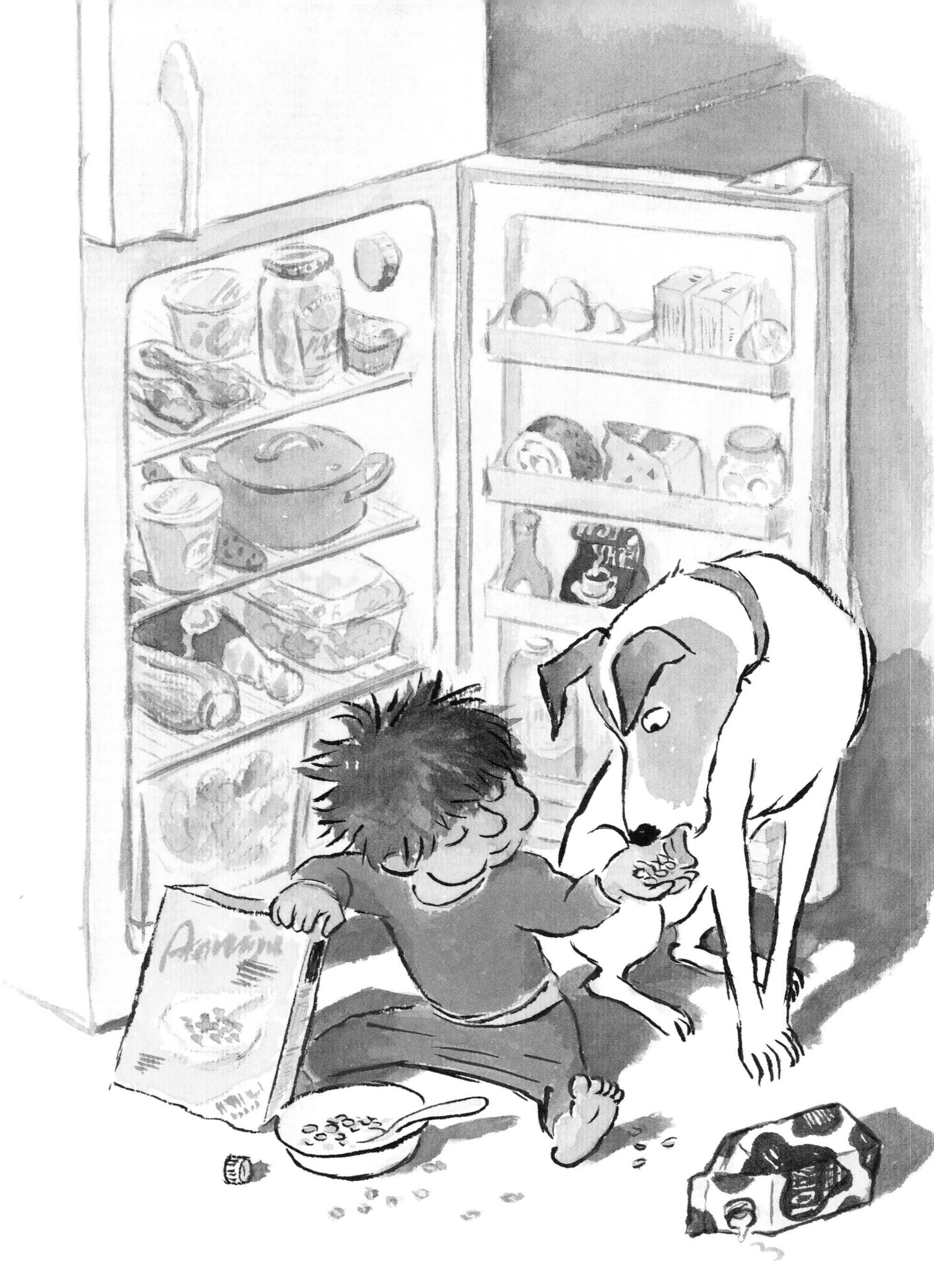

Behind a door, I find a feast
and share it with a hairy beast.

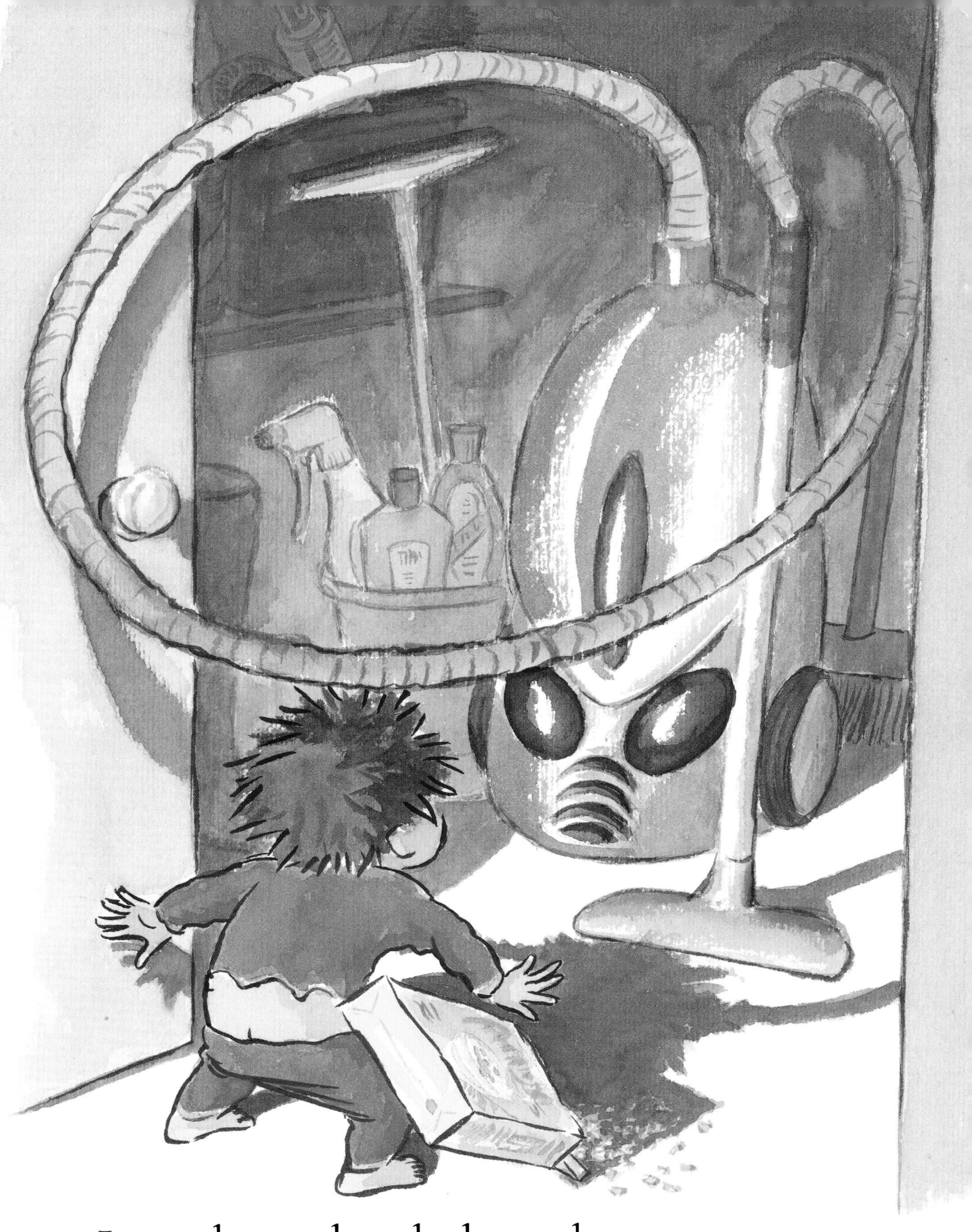

I sneak inside a hiding place,
confront a monster face-to-face.

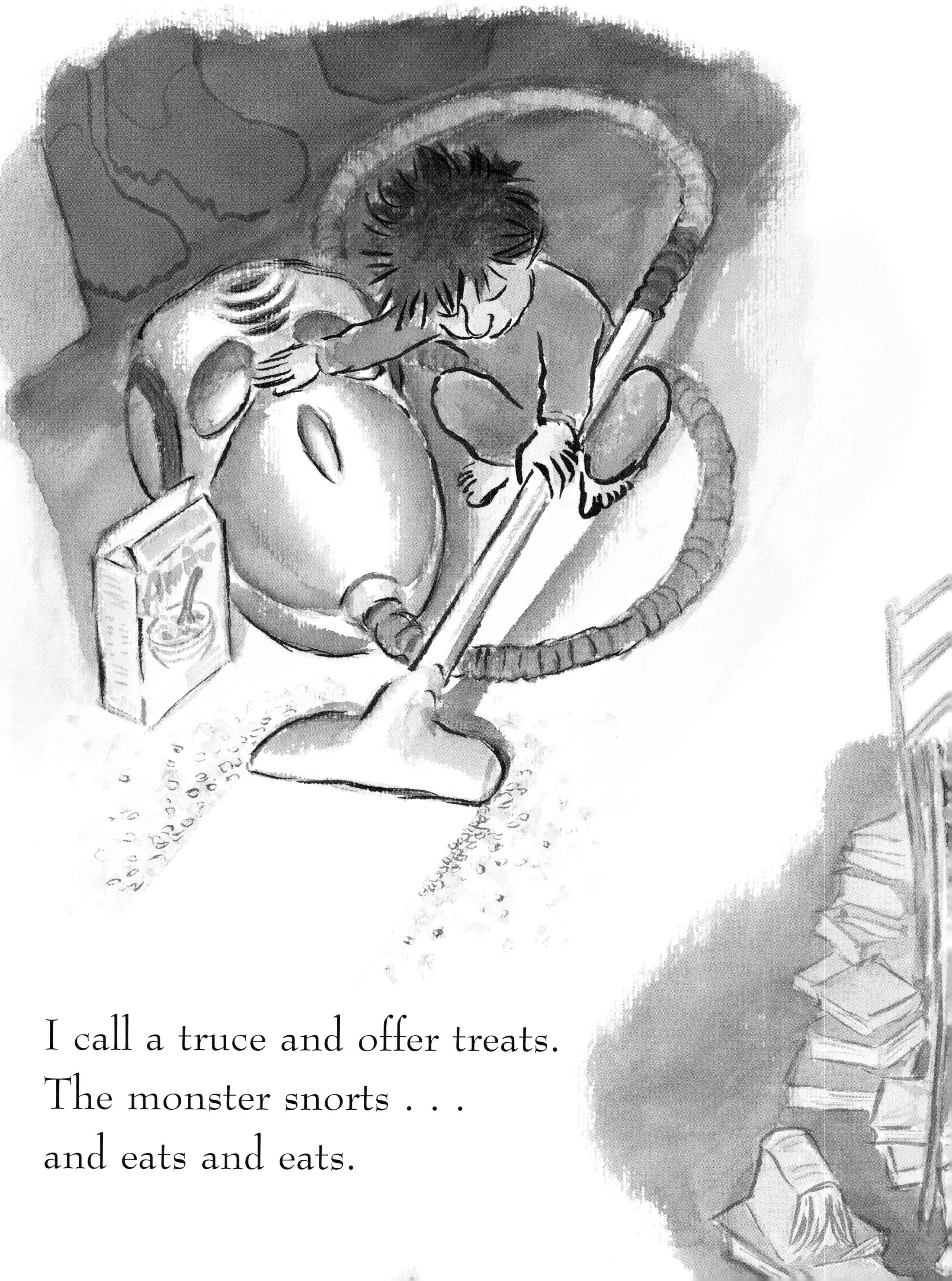

I call a truce and offer treats.
The monster snorts . . .
and eats and eats.

I build a castle on a ridge,
dig a moat, construct a bridge,
free a dragon from its crate,
post the creature at the gate.

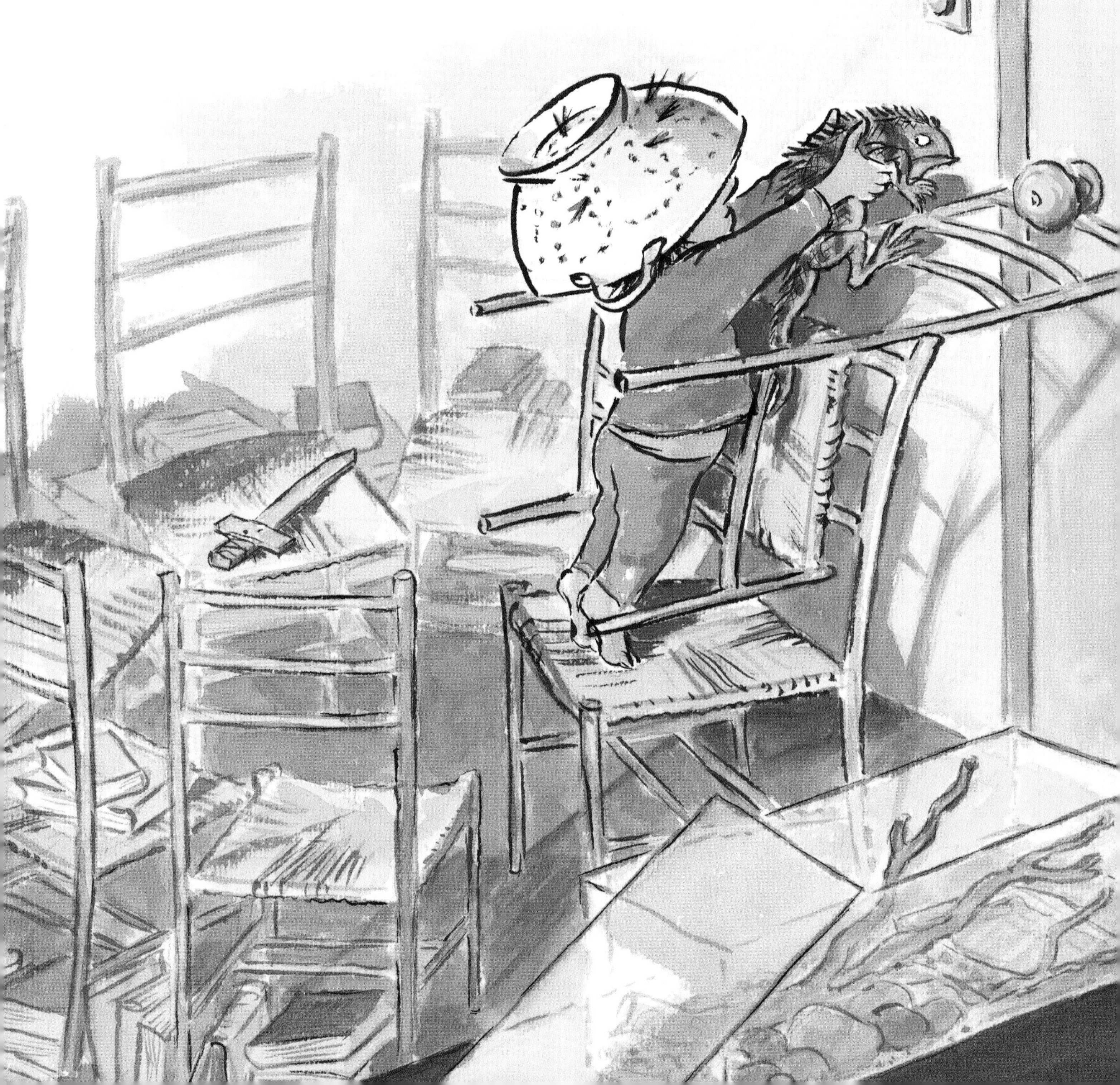

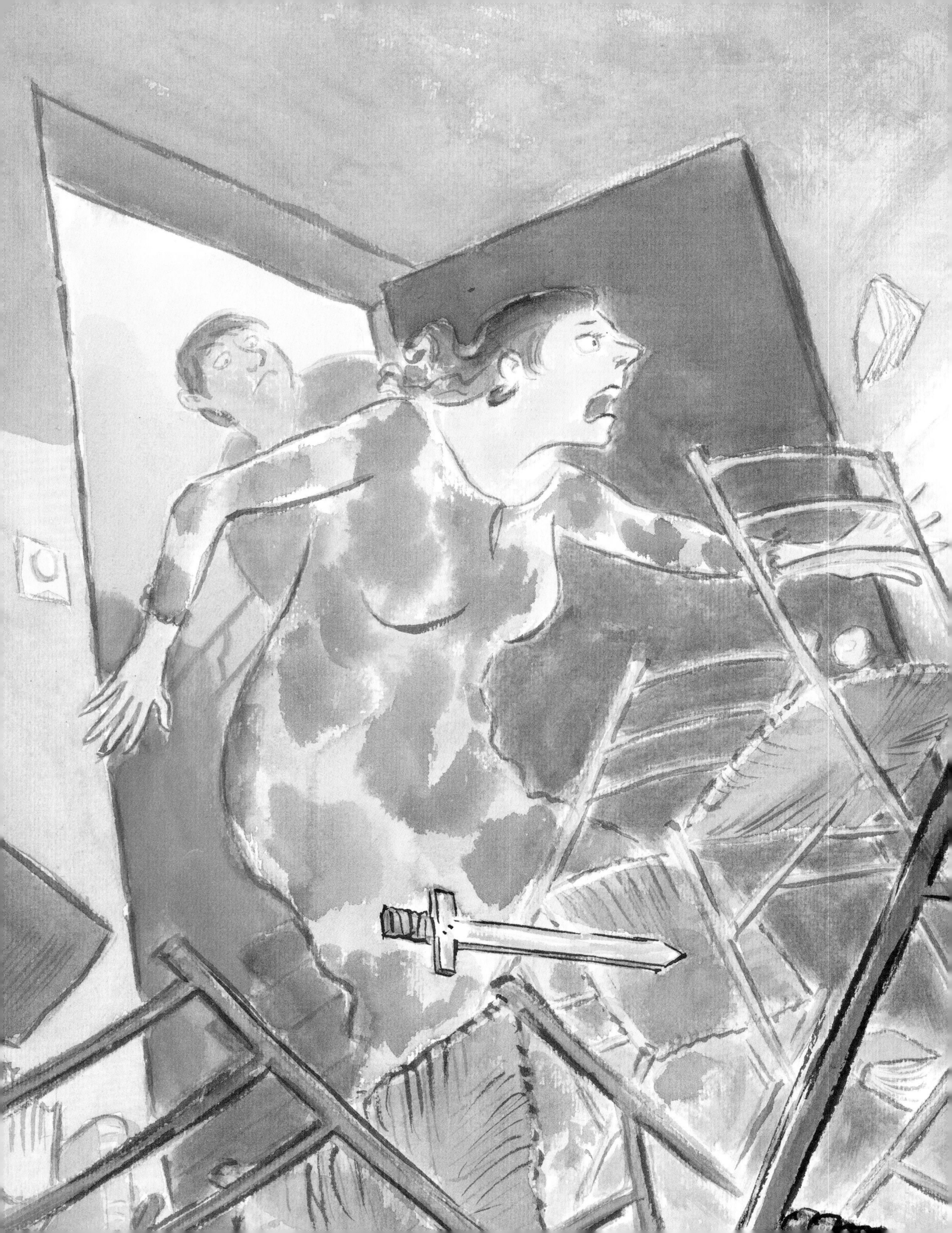

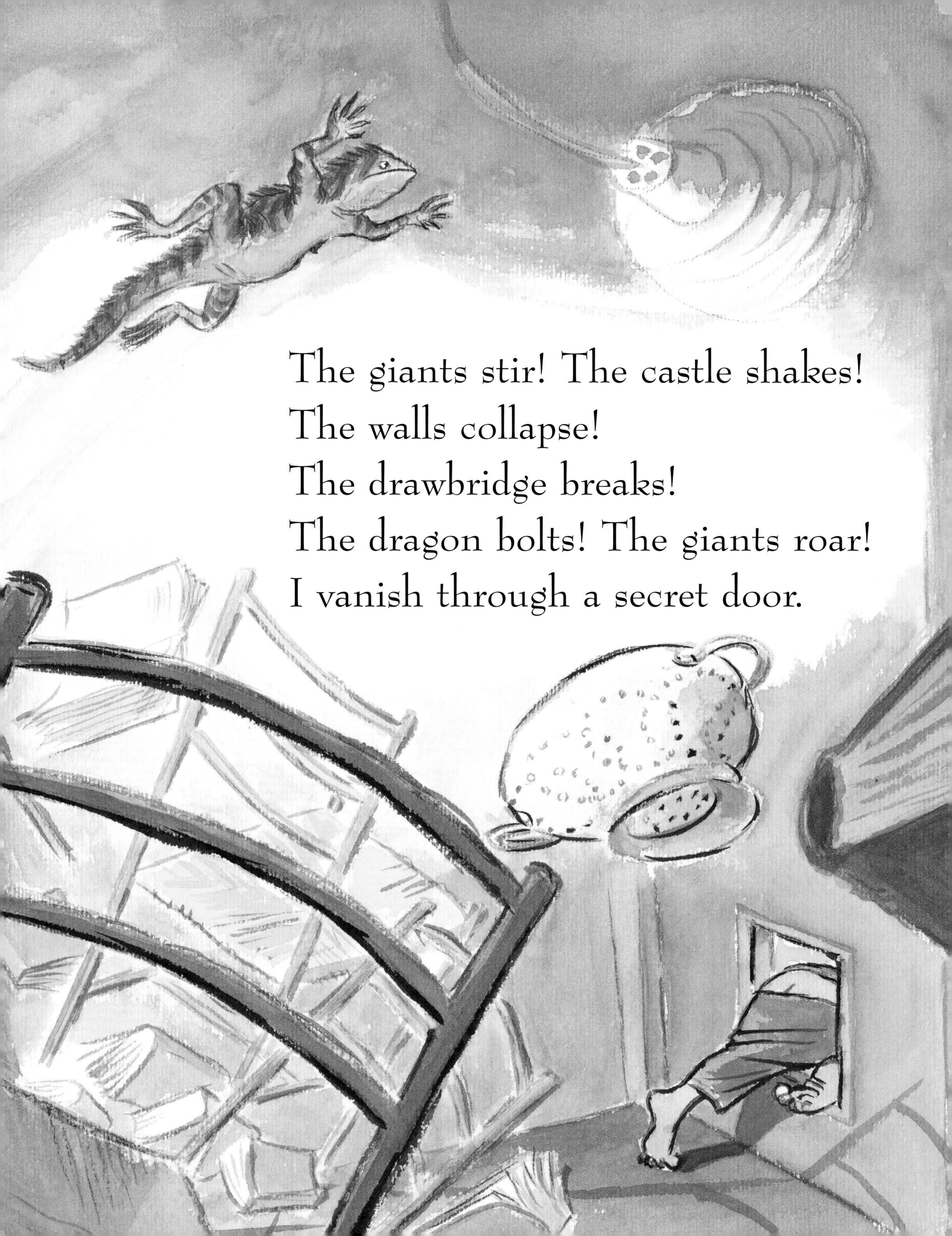

The giants stir! The castle shakes!
The walls collapse!
The drawbridge breaks!
The dragon bolts! The giants roar!
I vanish through a secret door.

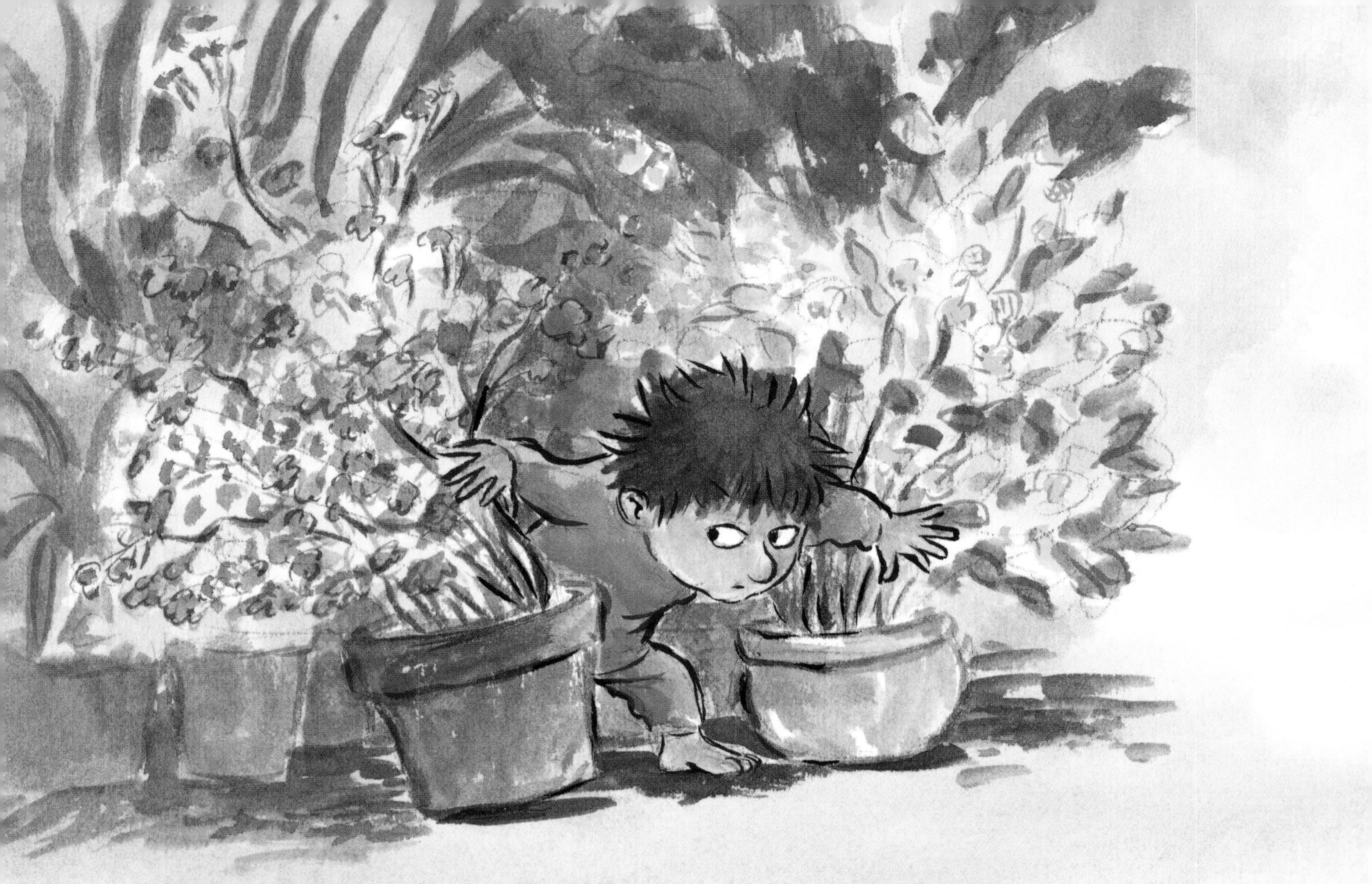

I cross a jungle, leap a lake,
wrestle with a spitting snake,

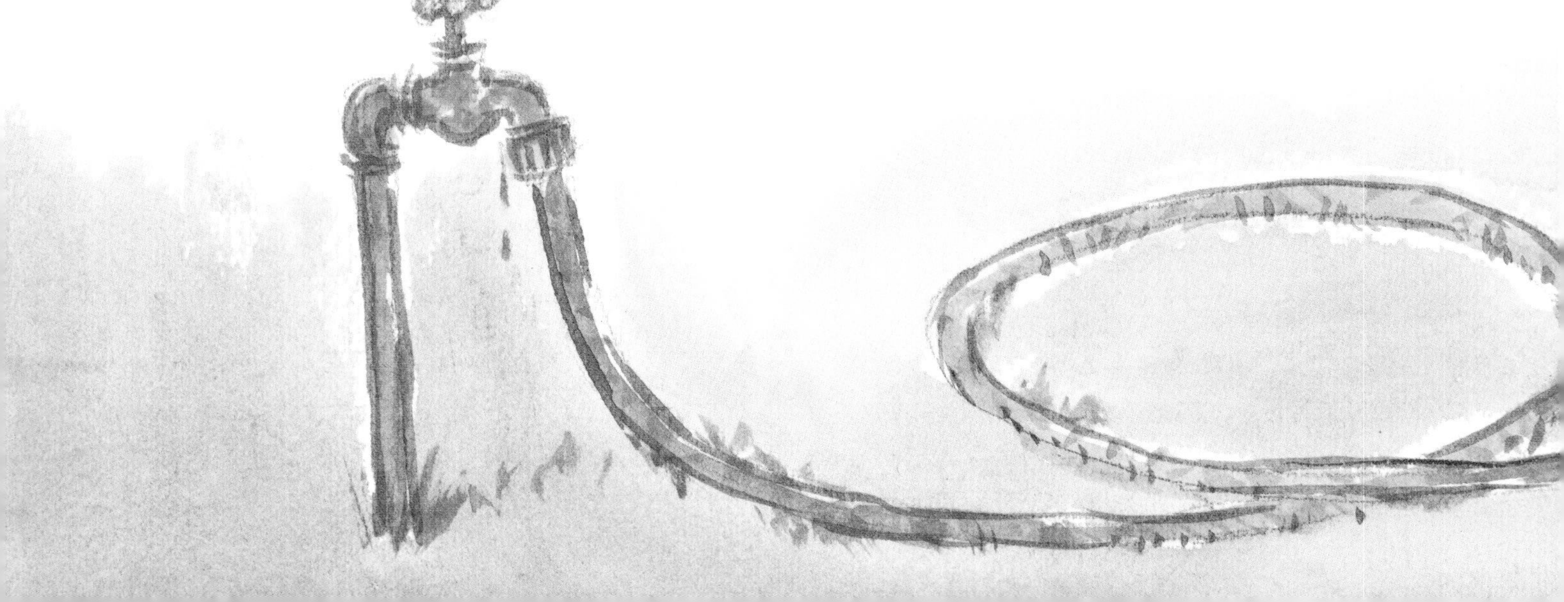

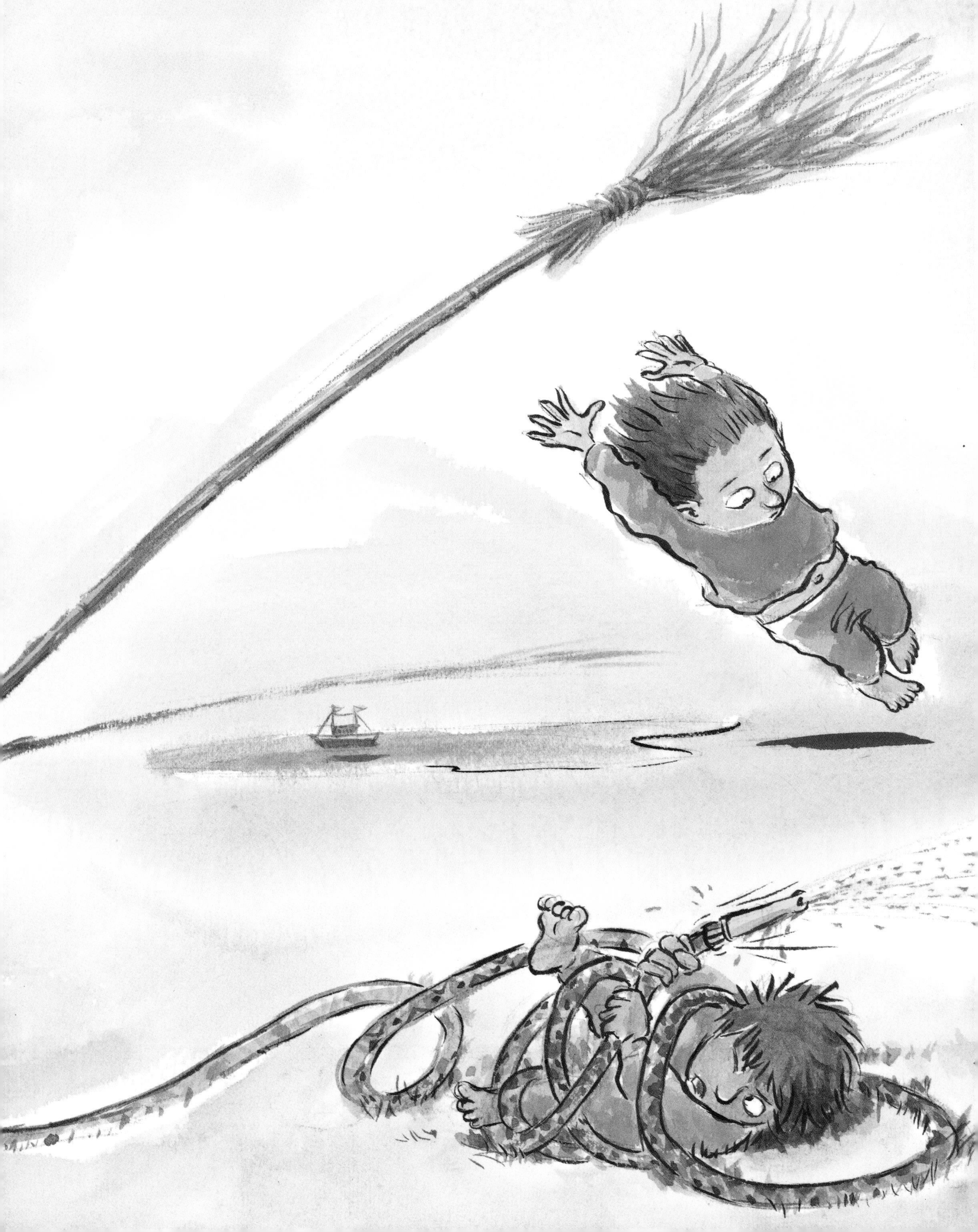

trek through desert,
crawl through caves,
sail a boat through tidal waves.

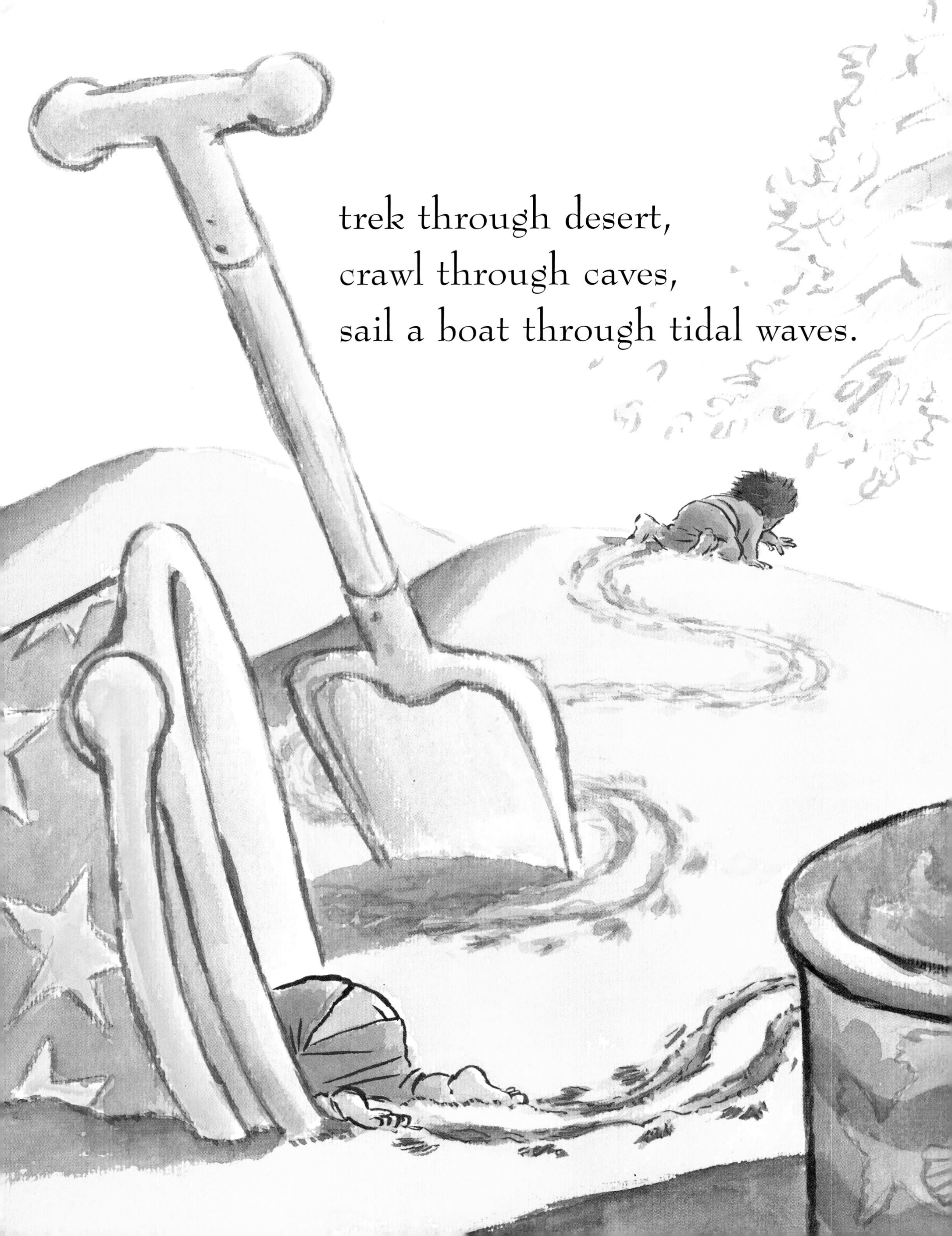

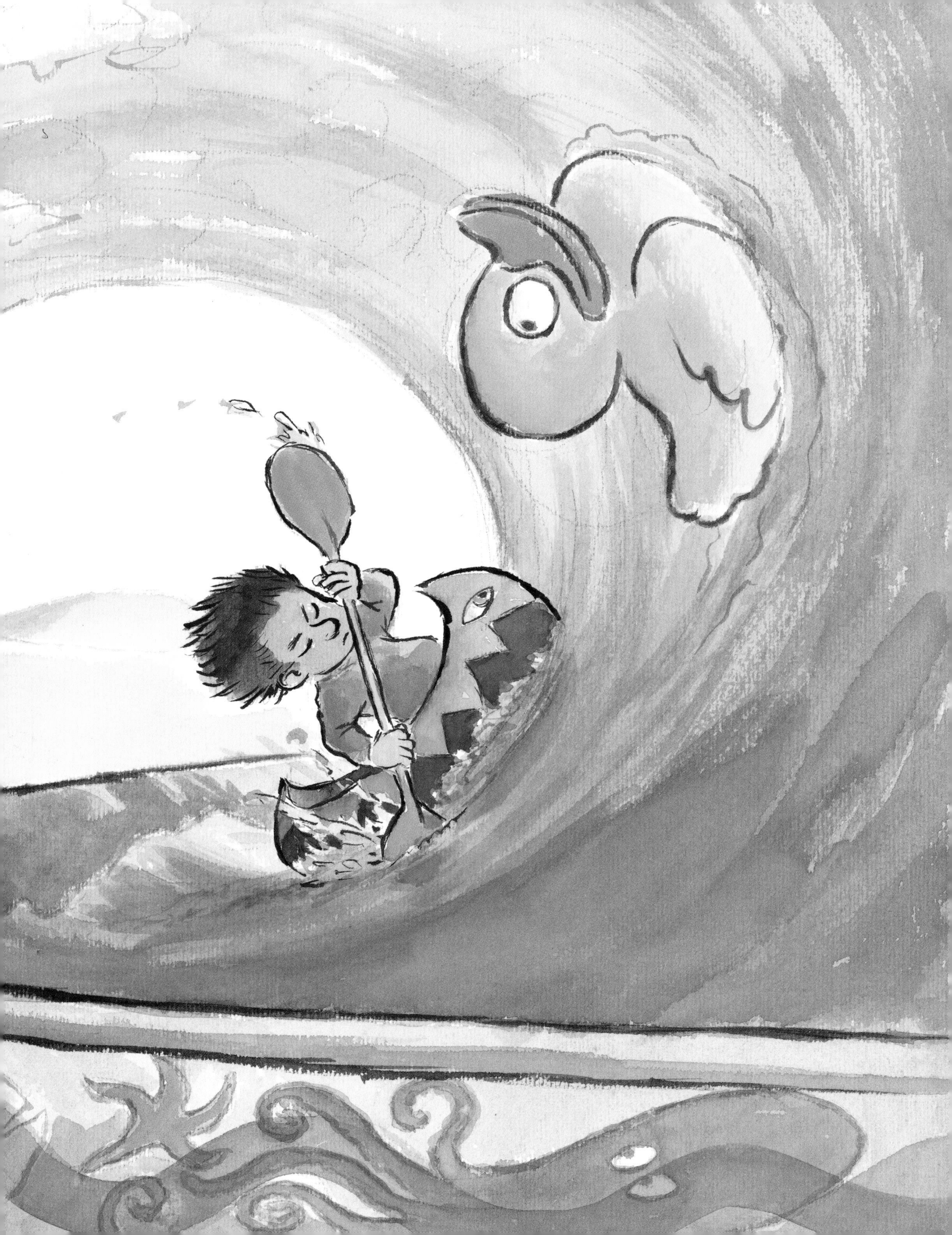

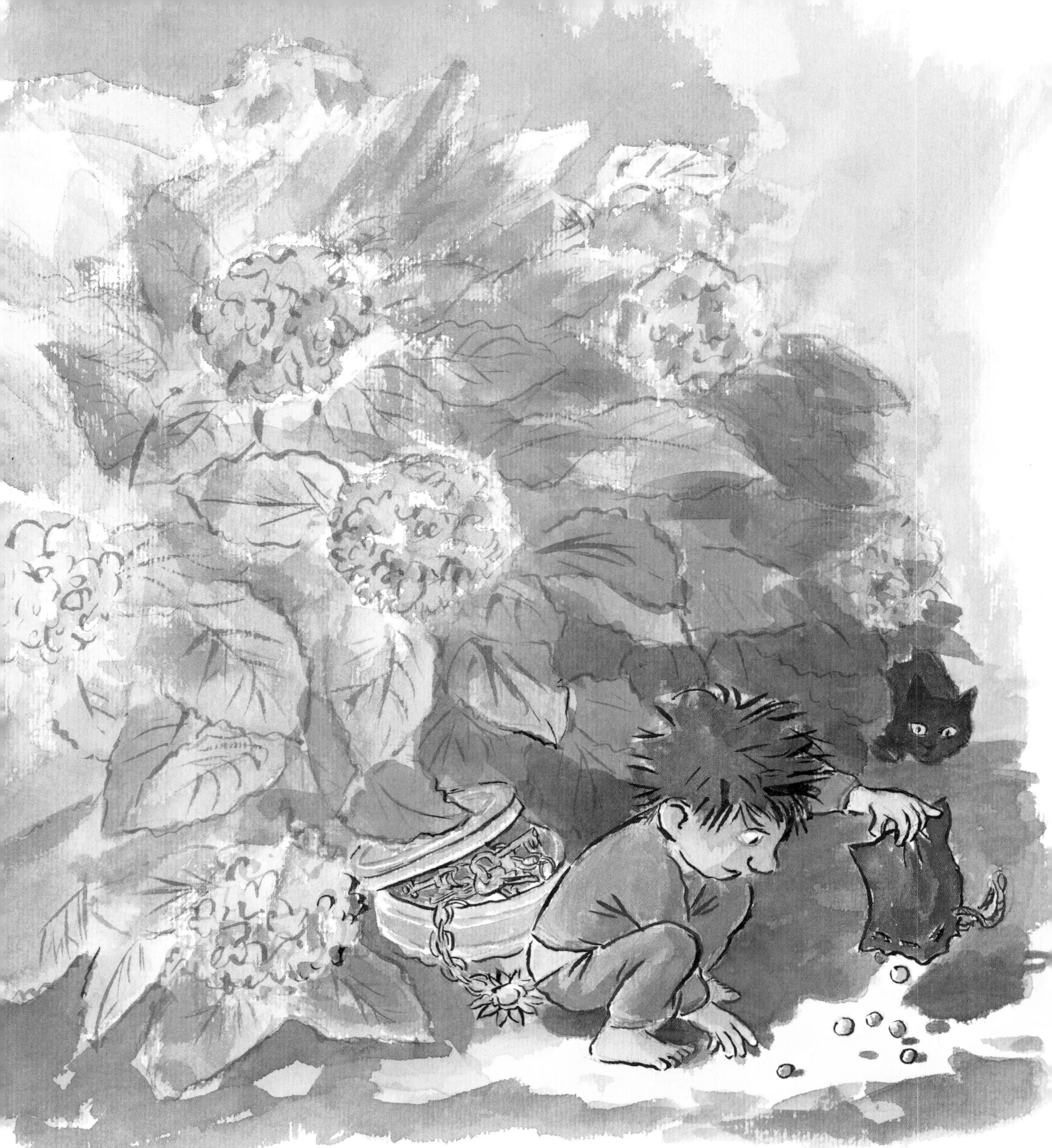

I find a bag of sparkling jewels,
then grab my finest mining tools.

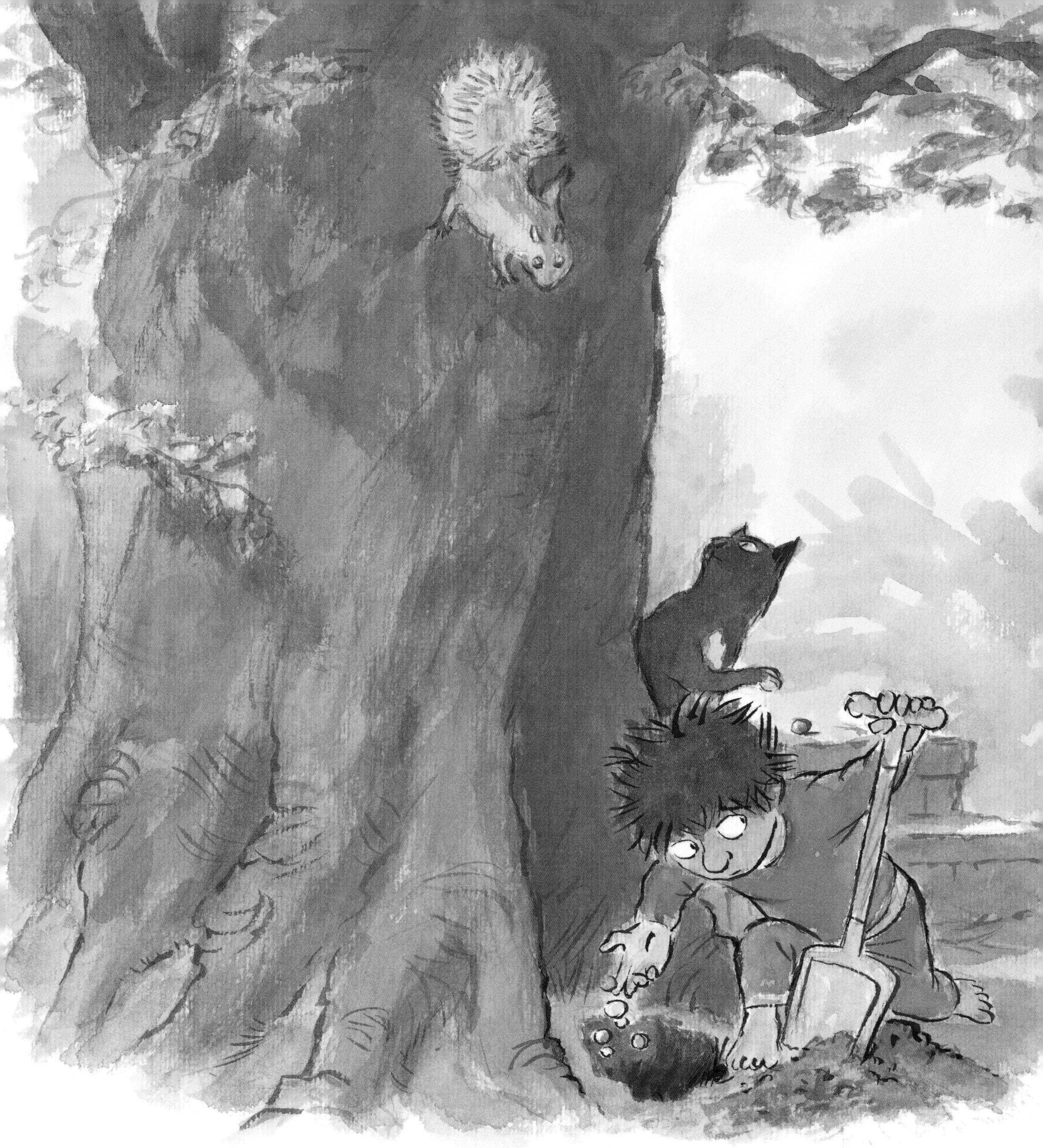

I dig a crevice dark and wide,
hide the treasure deep inside.

I join a traveling circus troupe,
teach a clown to hula-hoop,
train a monkey, tame a cat,
tumble like an acrobat.

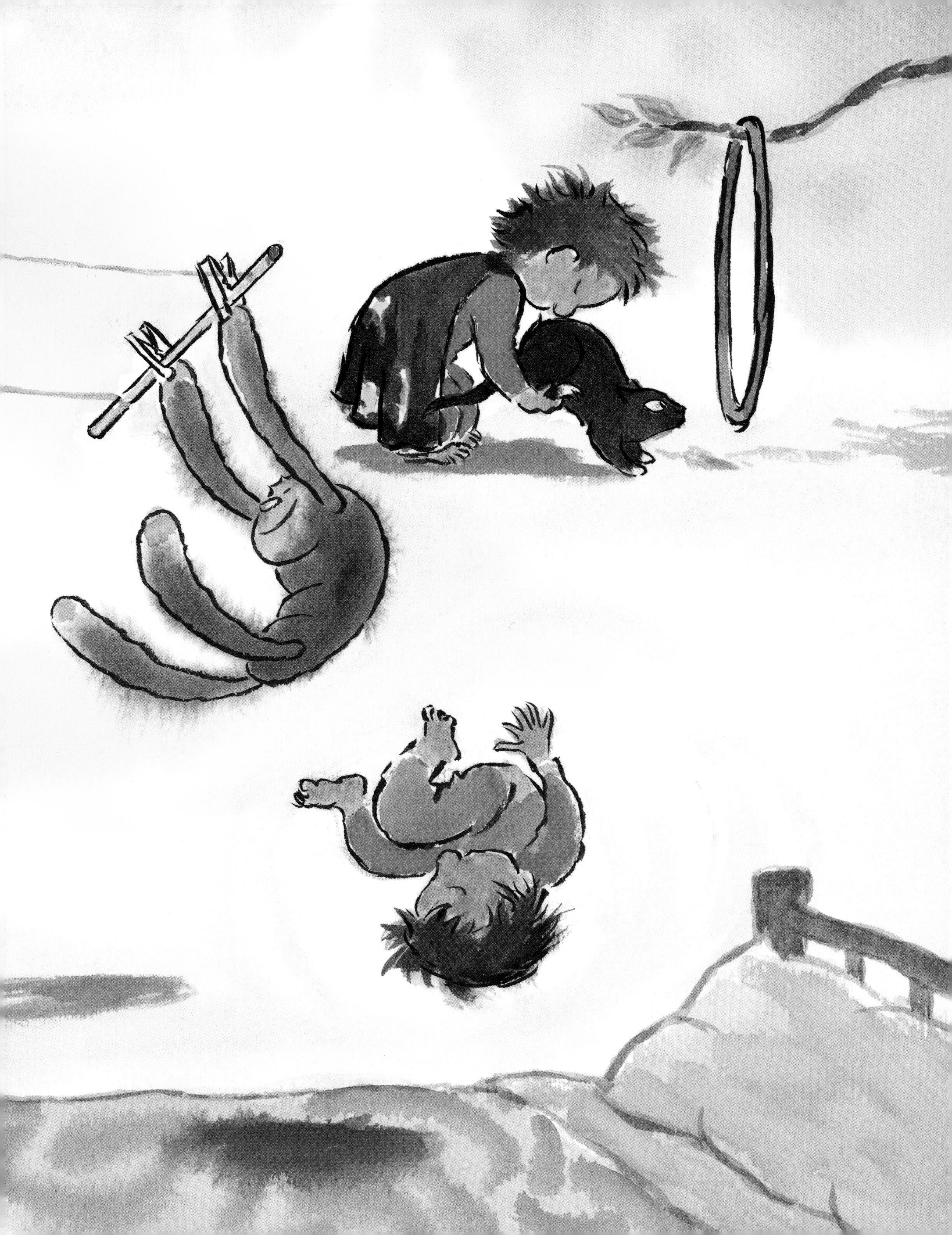

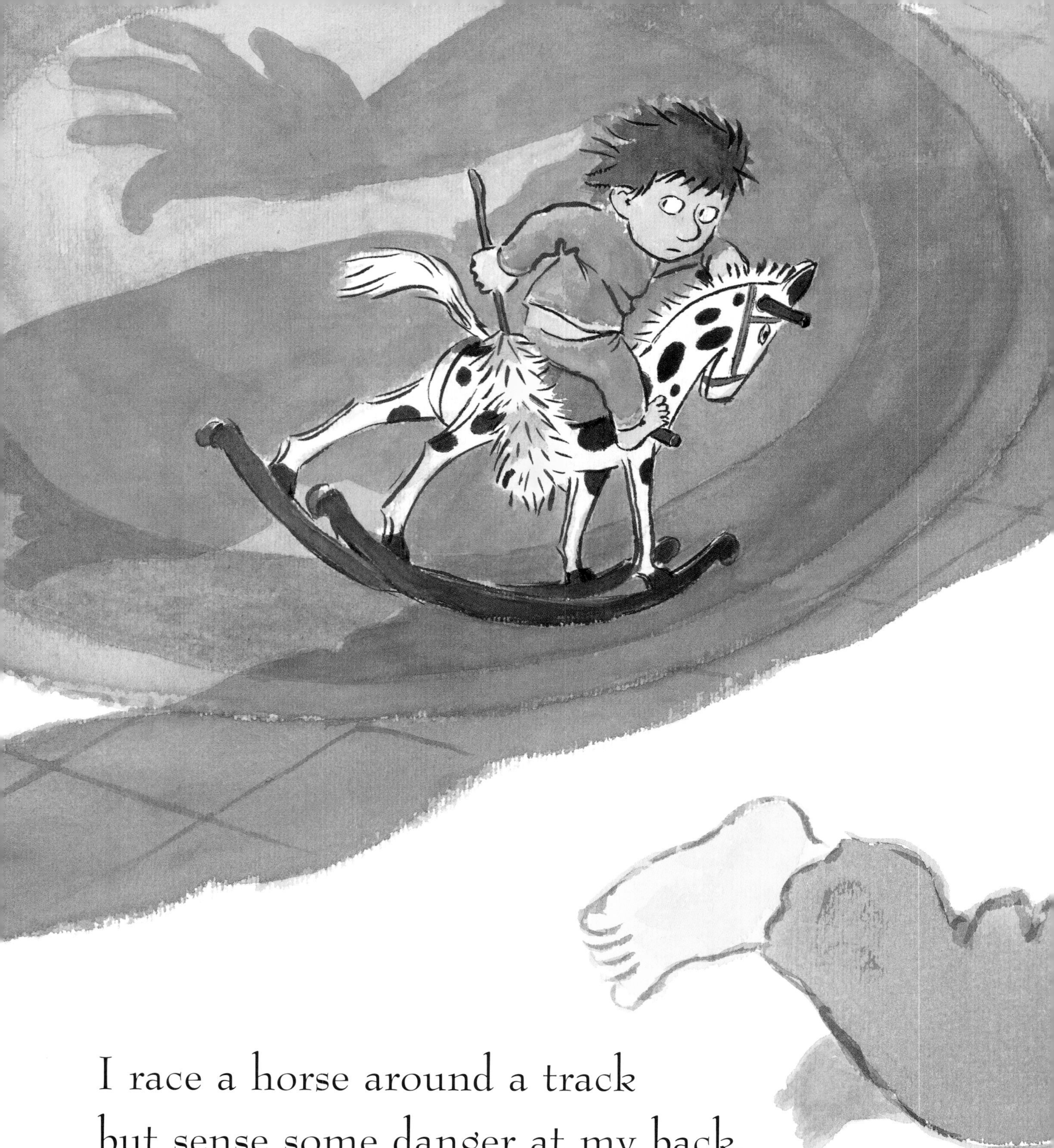

I race a horse around a track
but sense some danger at my back.
I turn—a giant's chasing me!
He scoops me up. I can't break free.

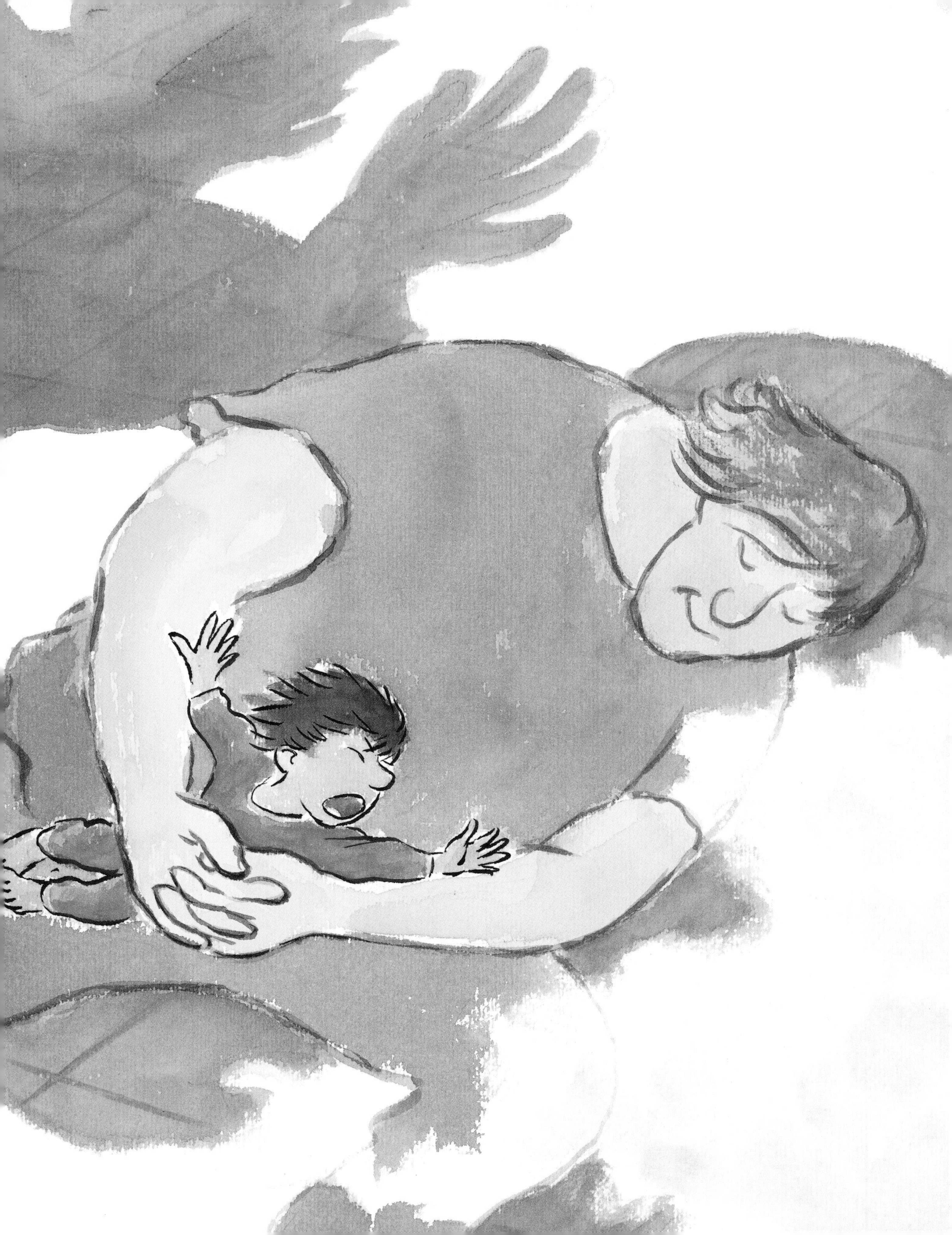

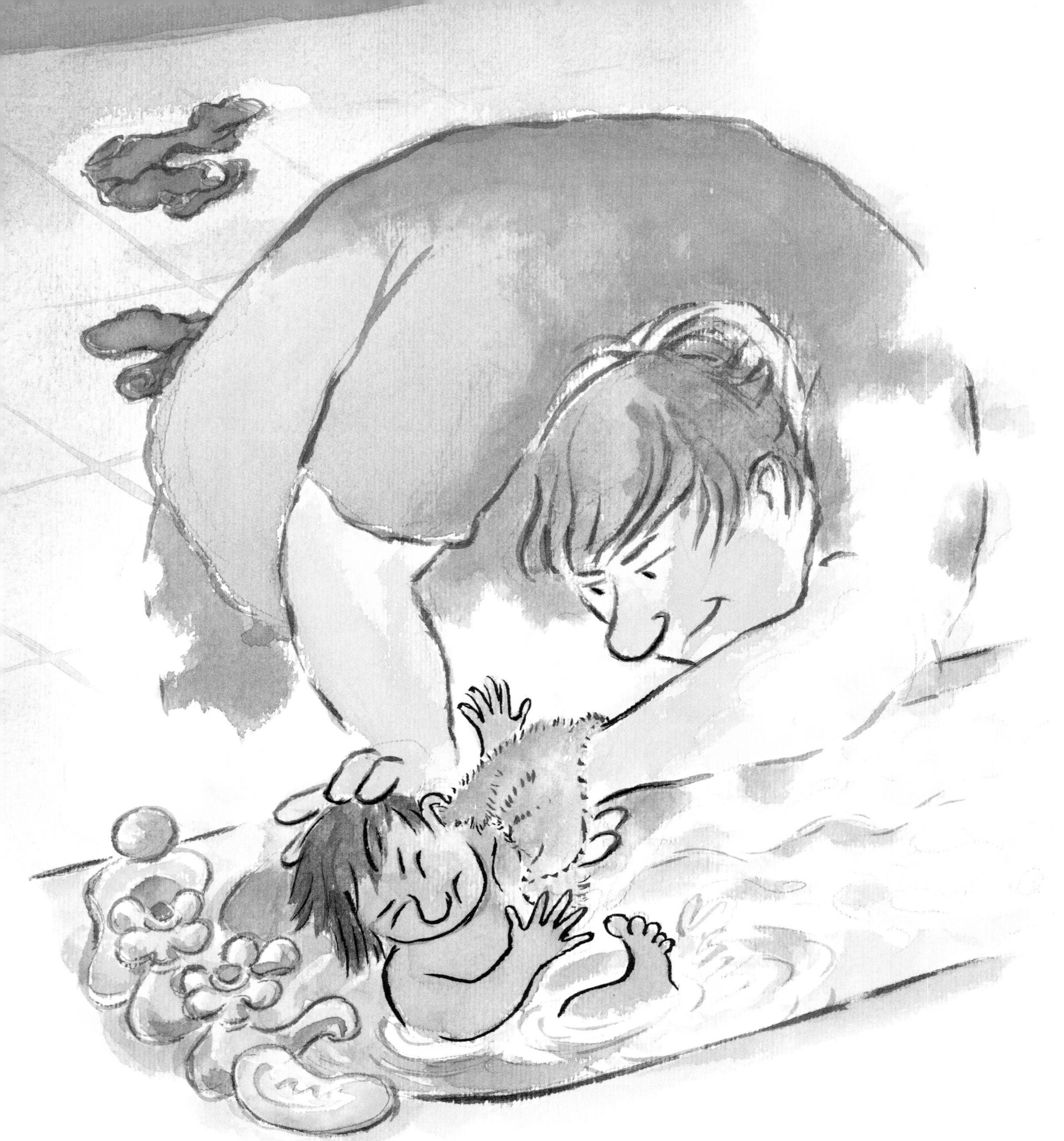

He dunks me in a bubbling tub,
makes me soak and scrape and scrub.

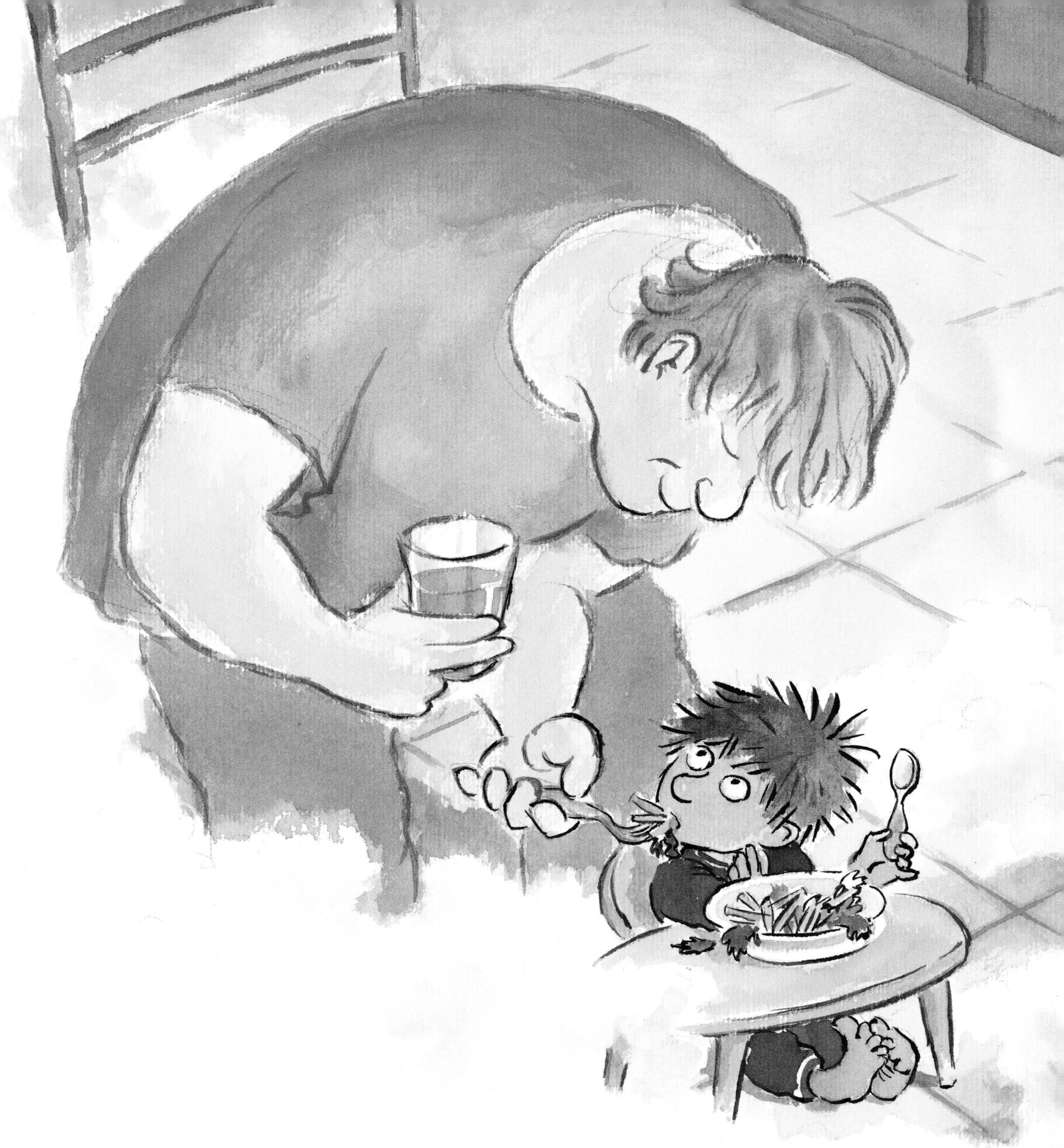

He feeds me sticks and weeds for lunch,
then gives me magic sleeping punch.

I drink the stuff. I stretch and yawn.
My legs are weak. My strength is gone.

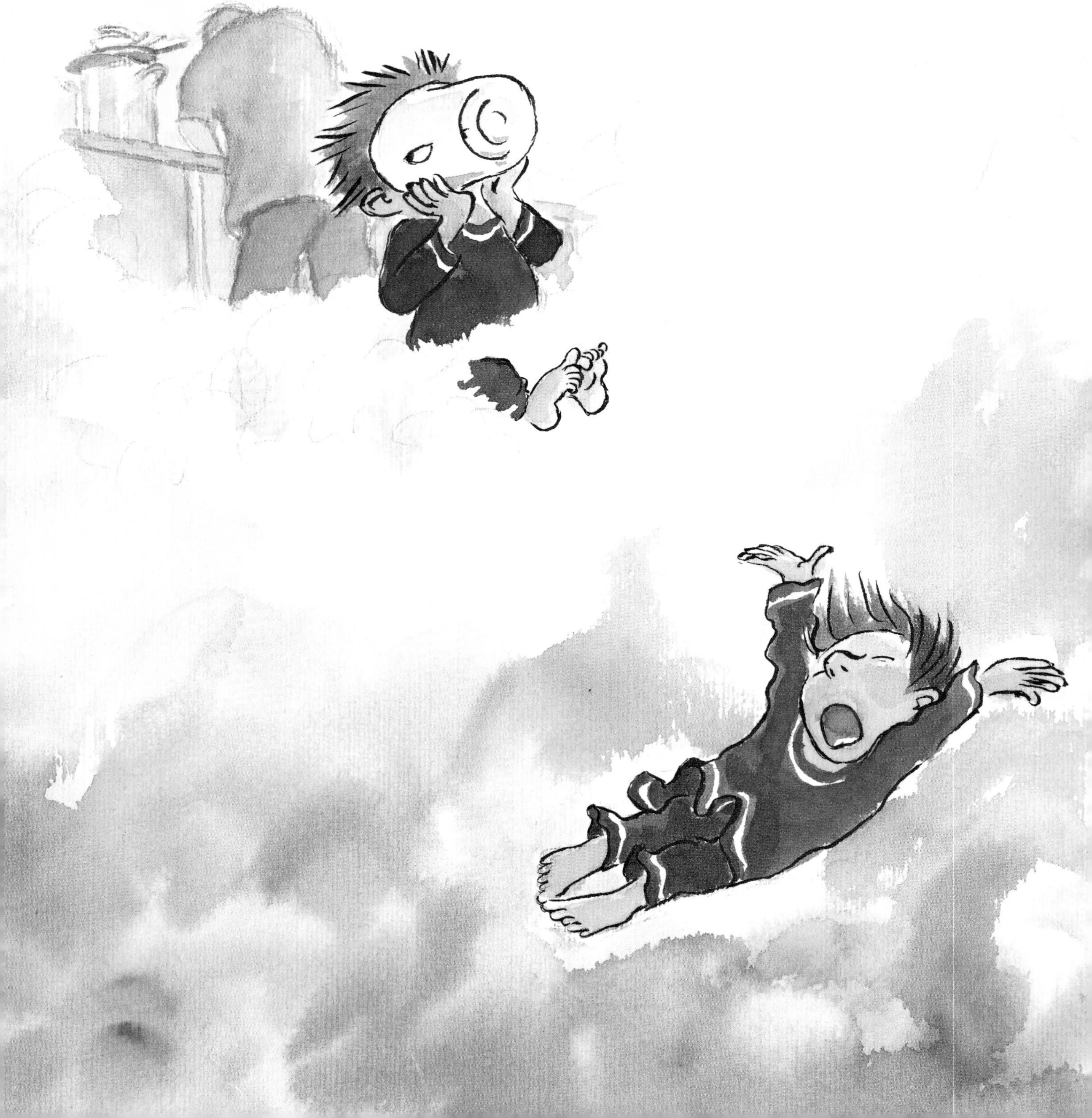

I fall into the giant's lap,
curl up tight . . .

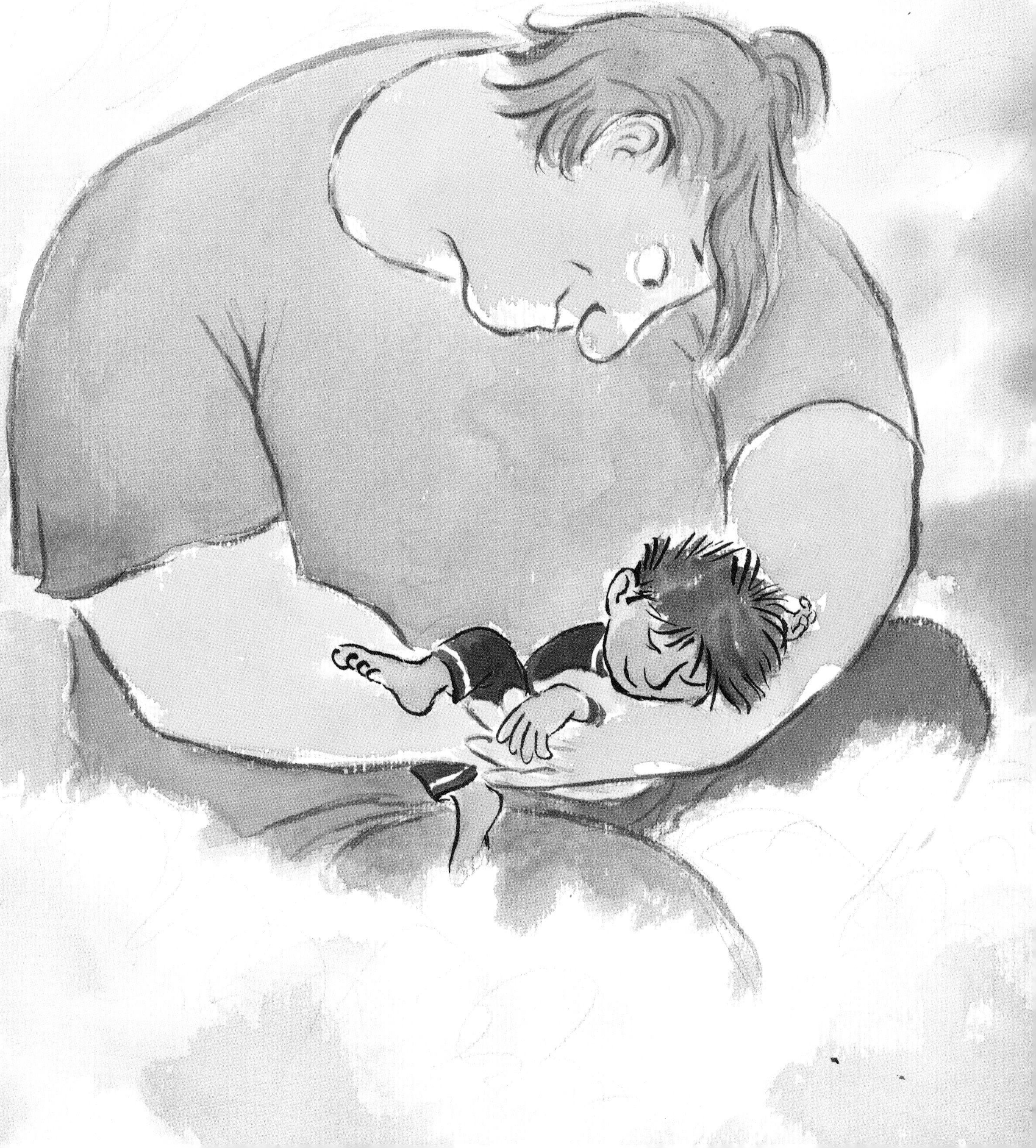

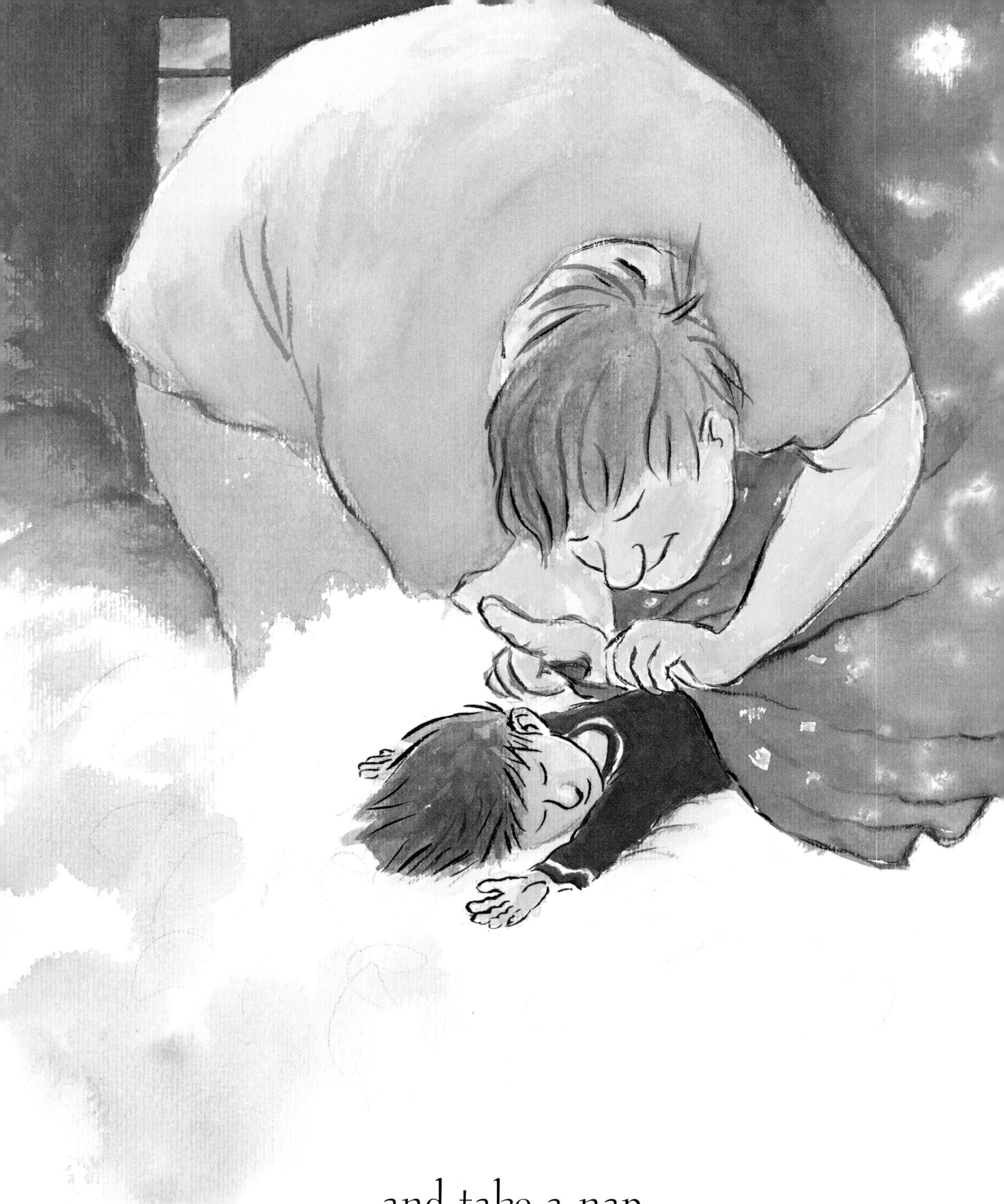

and take a nap.

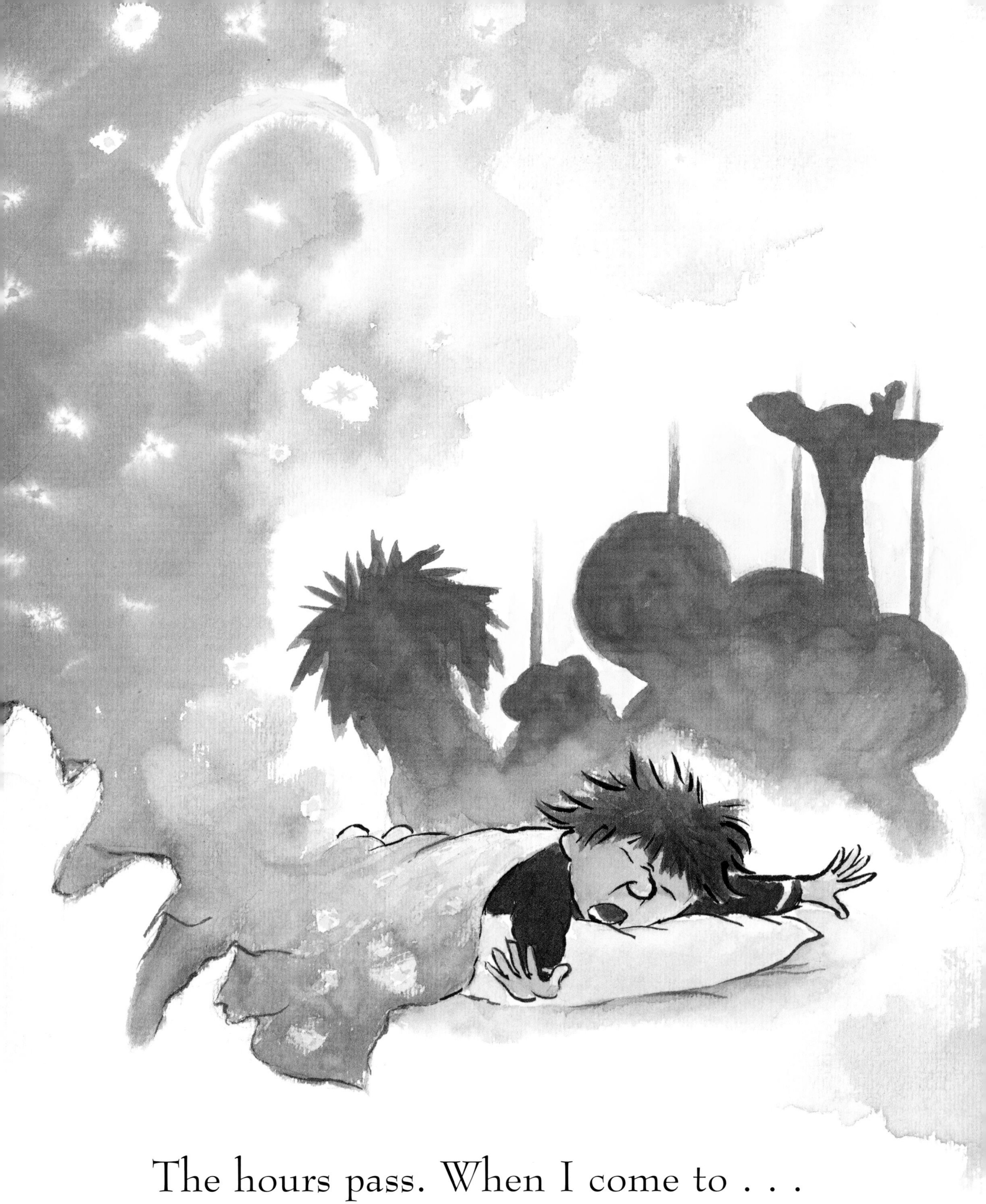

The hours pass. When I come to . . .

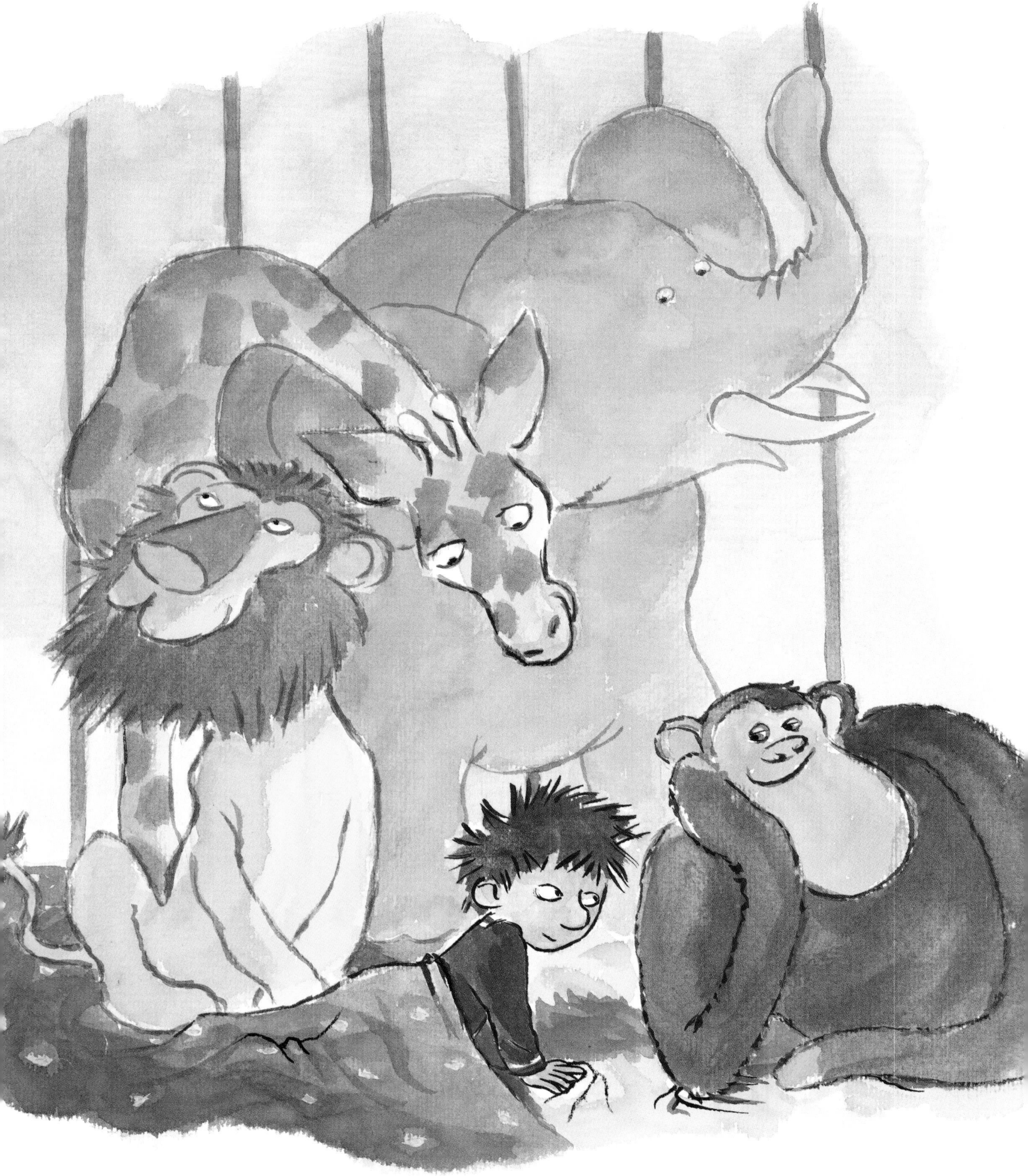

I find myself inside a zoo. . . .